From Everything
to Nothing
and Back

Mairi Speirs

Elephant
Chance

Published in 2018 by Elephant Chance

ISBN Paperback: 978-1-9164541-0-1
Ebook: 978-1-9164541-1-8

A CIP catalogue copy of this book can be
found in the British Library.

Published with the help of Indie Authors World
indieauthorsworld.com

IndieAuthors
World

For my family with love, Mairi

Reviews

'I was hooked from the very first page. Mairi captures the essence of how the ripple effect of one rash decision can affect the lives of so many as the story unfolds like the workings of a great tapestry. The unholy mess on one side revealing the most beautiful picture on the other.

' The devastation and loss for the women who had to give up their child but the joy and thankfulness bestowed on those who received them. I couldn't put this book down!'

Liz Thorburn, Author of Where's Nessie

'This debut novella by Mairi Speirs is a painfully, honest tale of a woman's life-long struggle to come to terms with being forced to give up her infant baby girl for adoption and the permanent gap of not knowing what happened to her daughter'.

'The story describes the turmoil faced by a pregnant young girl and her family in Ceylon who insisted on the baby being adopted. It's a pacy read, which gives a sharp insight into the key issues that dominated and shaped the woman's life thereafter'.

'From Everything to Nothing and Back points up some uncomfortable truths and adds further reality to an already distressing topical issue'.

Anne Clarke

As our unforgiving society seeks forgiveness and our cold echoing churches seek warmth this beautiful new book from Mairi Speirs is both timely and insightful.

In the story Sam, the gentle cafe owner, seats the reader at a table just across the room from a sad woman they do not know called Nadia who was forced to give up her child in the 60's.

This fictional novella, from everywhere to nothing and back is tragic and heartbreaking and yet, it is heart warming too.

Tommy Sands

Life is no brief candle to me. It is a sort of splendid torch which I have got hold of for the moment, and I want to make it burn as brightly as possible before handing it on to future generations

George Bernard Shaw

Introduction

What happened to the women who were forced to give up their children for adoption in the 1960s? Was it as simple as putting pen to paper? No. Did they ever discover whether it was a happy or sad journey for their child? Many didn't And what happened to the mums once they signed the papers? Many of them felt helpless once the authorities had what they wanted. Here, Nadia, Sam, Maria, and others, tell their heart-rending stories.

Chapter 1

Memories

I feel such a longing to be back in Ceylon, with all the family sitting round the table. I imagine and pretend the homecoming of the 'prodigal' daughter. Have they fattened a lamb?

Will my father even be alive now? Could he run to greet me? I feel so sad that I still seek forgiveness after all this time, still hoping he might say, 'Come home, all is forgiven.' That ship sailed long ago. Yet the longing remains at certain times.

What a foolish old woman I am. I can still smell the familiar smells of my childhood home, particularly the aroma of freshly-made tea. Such a strong memory has never been erased, even though it was so long ago.

Those feelings are triggered again today as I enter the Cinnamon Café. Noticing that it's unusually busy, I look around for a vacant seat. It must be the milder weather that has brought so many people outdoors.

Spotting an empty table near the window, I sit down then glance round the café without really taking any real notice of who is there. I take my glasses out of my bag, then place it under the seat and wait to give my order.

The café owner, Sam, is smiling as he stands by the counter. He glances in my direction, and I wonder if he notices that we are of a similar age. As he gathers his notepad and walks over to take my order, I admire how well dressed and distinguished he looks, with his neatly-cut silver hair.

'Hello, how are you today?' he asks politely.

'Good,' I reply, trying to feign a smile which does not quite reach my eyes. 'And you?'

'I am very well, thank you. What can I get you?'

'A cup of tea, please. And could you make it extra strong?'

'Of course.' He scribbles something on his pad, before looking up again. 'Would you like to try our new range of scones? We have just started selling them this week – apple and cinnamon?'

'Hmm.' He waits patiently while I pretend to consider the suggestion, then eventually I reply, 'No thank you. Just my tea.'

As I wait for my tea to arrive, my mind wanders and I begin to reminisce. I have been coming to this same cafe for over 40 years, and have seen two other owners come and go. But in the past few years, I have particularly warmed to the current owners. Yet I cannot put my finger on why. The others were always pleasant, but the couple who run it now are friendly and chatty – though not overly so. No prying questions that go beyond interested to being nosey. Just a genuine interest in making all their customers feel welcome.

The sound of laughter jolts me back to my current surroundings, and I smile in thanks as my order is set out neatly on my small table. The smell of the strong tea wafting up from my cup sends a message to my brain. I involuntarily lift it, sip it, then return it to the saucer.

Today, my lunch break has brought me here. Another day it might be a morning tea break. Or a detour on my way home. I come and go once or twice a week, sometimes every day, depending on my schedule or disposition.

As I slowly sip my tea, I relax and begin to look at the customers around me. People-watching evokes a feeling of happiness, as though I am part of something – even if it is on the periphery. I have learned to feel secure in this building, even for a short period of time.

At a nearby table is a young family. I smile, but no interaction is forthcoming. The adults appear harassed.

'Can you get them?' the woman asks the man in an irritated voice.

She is trying to sound polite but sounds angry. She turns to the wide-eyed children and asks why they brought bats, balls, dolls, golf clubs. There is no reply.

The man tells them, 'Next time, you both choose one thing each, do you hear me? This,' he points to various items at the side of their chairs, 'is not happening again. As usual, Mum and I are left to carry everything.'

I overhear the word picnic, and think how I used to love the ones we had back home so many years ago. I feel the tears prick behind my eyes, and blink quickly to push them back. I stiffen my shoulders and quietly scold myself: *You are a grown woman. You cannot let your emotions out now, so stop this nonsense in public.* I take a deep breath to avert any attention, as I know that would be too embarrassing. I feel the anger rise and push it back to where it must stay. I cannot allow it to become public. It is a private matter.

After about half an hour, I get up slowly and organise myself in a fraction of the time the family takes to gather up their belongings. At the till, I quietly ask to pay for my tea and hand over my debit card, while pretending to search in my bag – anything to avoid eye contact with the owner while he rings up my payment.

I know I have had better days, but I have had many worse too. And I must continue to believe this to survive. I politely take my change and receipt, before leaving the cafe.

Once outside, I breathe in the fresh air and give myself another talking-to. *Right, Nadia, onwards and upwards. You must get through this week; you still have November to face.*

Despite enjoying my visit to the café, the uneasiness has started, and I struggle to control what can only be compared to living with the constant feeling of rising 'bile' prior to being physically sick.

Chapter 2

The Cinnamon Café

The 15th of November is here again. With every passing year, this painful date burns at my very core. In my late sixties, I sit alone in a café in London, looking out at the driving rain so often associated with British winters. Through the window, I watch a young woman of about 24 as she makes her way across the busy street. She appears to be in a hurry, glances quickly at her watch, slows down, then enters the café.

I start to wonder why she is in such a rush. Work commitments? Is she en route to a liaison? Who would know? Is everyone just easily going about their own business? How would you know?

She is a tall, well-dressed girl whose expression reveals nothing to an observer. But perhaps she is displaying the stiff upper lip, historically synonymous with the middle and upper classes within British society. I know this approach only too well. It rudely translates to presenting one persona on the surface, while on the inside your spirit may be broken beyond repair without anyone ever suspecting a thing.

My musings are interrupted by the cheerful tone of the proprietor, Sam Anderson, as he jovially tries to interact with his latest customer.

'Well, hello there.'

'Hi,' she replies tonelessly.

'It's good to see you again. Where have you been hiding? What can I get for you today?' His friendliness is undeterred by her response.

'A coffee, strong. Very strong,' she says, still without expression.

I'm perplexed as I overhear her order. I wonder if she just likes her coffee strong, or if something has happened. Has she been up all night and needs a 'booster', maybe? I realise I will never know, but it doesn't stop a jumble of thoughts from occurring.

'No problem, coming right up,' says Sam, but his joviality is lost on the young woman.

Sam Anderson is the man whose name appears above the door of the Cinnamon Café. He is a kind man; a railwayman's son who hails from the east coast of Scotland. I only know this because I overheard him telling one of the other customers some time ago. In his early sixties, he appears to be of Eastern descent, with his swarthy complexion, greying hair, and beard.

I find comfort in this jolly man, but that is not the main reason I continue to come here regularly. Having lived nearby for many, many years since the fateful day which was to change my life forever, I find some comfort in the familiarity of Richmond-upon-Thames. Indifference has been replaced by an acceptance, rather than a love of it.

This café feels safe. It smells of freshly ground coffee and baking bread. The food cabinet is pristine, and each tray is filled with appealing food, sitting to attention waiting for the next customer to disturb the orderly rows. If I was hungry, I would find myself dithering over what to choose; it all looks so tasty. There is a good balance of wood and glass which brings a sense of warmth to the room, but unfortunately not today. The rain, slamming against the glass, sounds cold and hard.

I look around, hopeful that the surroundings may invoke some small sense of calm, as relaxing as the décor is on the eyes. For a brief moment, my mind wanders. The walls are painted in a soft caramel and vanilla, almost the shade of the cream placed on top of the scones. This is contrasted by a very pale pistachio green, which instantly reminds me of young life. Not human life, but rather that of the young foliage in Kew Gardens which blossoms in springtime.

The tables complement the décor to perfection, with a mixture of oval, square, and rectangular shapes, whereby the subtle buttermilk and honey finish depicts class and sophistication. I begin to relax as I exhale quietly, then once again question what it is that keeps bringing me back here. Is it my need to feel some form of comfort? Or to evoke the kind of calmness I have learned to present as I go about my everyday life. These serene surroundings, which have become so familiar, hold a special meaning for me. But I cannot fathom why.

As I stare out of the window, in the distance I catch sight of the church steeple. I shudder as I visualise the 'heath' beyond my vision, with its large expanse of land, shops, restaurants, and hotels. A community place where many families gather on Sundays to respect the traditional day of rest, where the traditional and modern mix. Older couples out for an afternoon walk before retiring to read the papers, then tucking into their 'proper' Sunday roast, unable to escape the tradition even though their children are all grown up and away.

Middle-aged couples, with more disposable income, enjoy the luxury of going out to enjoy brunch in one of the local eateries; a treat which was unaffordable for previous generations. They saved and saved, while others threw caution to the wind and opted to drive their up-to-date cars with their personal registrations. How many of them did it to 'paper over the cracks', using consumerism to feed a 'gap' which society promoted? Who will ever know?

Then there are some just wanting to spend Sunday 'quality' time with their families. I have long since realised that family structure has changed dramatically for subsequent generations; it's now so diverse and multicultural that I wonder about its value. I neither agree nor disagree, but I have felt the full emotional impact of an unforgiving society.

What power did the church have in society? I remember with a feeling of terror the church steeple 'standing to attention', having provided many generations with a definitive line of acceptable standards. Why was there never any forgiveness or compassion shown? Despite the many challenges faced by the younger members of the congregation, I know all too well what could happen should you sway in any way against their unremitting code of conduct. The magnitude endured could not compete with any Richter scale.

My own upbringing enforced this message so strongly. I remember so clearly how the clergymen greeted parishioners, 'Welcome, everyone... my sermon today is about...' Followed by a tirade which sparked a ripple of fear that permeated at the front and spread from one person to the next, almost like an airborne virus which affected everyone but no-one wanted to catch.

God have mercy on you if you caught it. Who really was welcome – the pristine, clean-cut, best dressed in the parish? No, don't be so ridiculous, Nadia, I chide myself. Well, everyone except the unwed, pregnant women. Although these words were never uttered, they were feared by so many innocent young women, who would brace themselves for the fallout bestowed upon sinners.

My body shudders again. Suddenly, I feel cold and my heart feels very heavy in my body.

'Hello. Hello. Hello,' I remember wanting to shout on one particular Sunday when I had gone to church to try to feel forgiveness. Sitting in the pew, I had looked around, thinking, how do you know who's pregnant and who is not?

The imaginary voice of the priest responded, 'God leads us to the sinners and we always find out who has sinned.' And I remember feeling foolish for thinking so vividly and wanting to shout out, 'Who said that?'

The sound of breaking glass startles me and jolts me back to my current surroundings. Sam is bending down to pick up the remains of what looks like a broken cup.

Adjusting myself on the seat until comfortable, I sigh then look down at the order I received about ten minutes ago. My apple and cinnamon scone, tea and honey, are cooling. I refocus as I take a bite and sip the tea. The subtle contrast of flavours explode in my mouth but do not register in my brain to produce the normal pleasurable experience. Why not?

I know so very well why. Today is the 15th of November, and I am still heartbroken. The pain is usually safely stored in my brain, but not today. I again retreat into my private world where I observe at least three franchise coffee shops on the other side of the road. I have often thought that perhaps I should give each of them my custom, to support them all. But somehow, the Cinnamon Café has always won. This 'one-off' coffee shop more than meets my requirements, and I hope it will for many more years to come.

Somewhere in the background, I hear the sound of laughter, which reminds me again why I like this café so much. On days like this, Sam leaves me alone to my own thoughts.

Where did that carefree girl go? What happened to her all those years ago? Why does it still ache like there's no tomorrow? Because on the 15th November 1960, my core was ripped from inside me – both literally and metaphorically.

I glance again at Sam Anderson and wonder, what would he have done all those years ago? I will never know. I will never ask him. I will never expose that sad lonely time in my life where I had no-one. Why would I? The people I trusted most in this world failed me. If I were to tell Sam, what would I say to him anyway? What would he think of me?

My mind is racing today; there are so many thoughts that I cannot suppress, regardless of how hard I try. How the mighty fall, I used to hear people say. Did I think I was mighty? No-one in my family did, even when my mother and I gazed in the department store window at displays, eagerly anticipating that season's fashion. I always wore it with grace and panache. I was always respectful of the privileged life I led. Even when I travelled on the *Orase* – a wonderful boat which took me to and from Southampton, transporting me from one luxurious lifestyle to another. Wined and dined, I was asked on many occasions, 'What can I get you to drink, Miss? Martini? Champagne?' Nadia sighed again. I did enjoy it some of the time.

Another random thought enters my mind as I suddenly recall once meeting a girl who looked so sad. She told me, 'Always remember, regardless of your social standing or the circumstances surrounding procreation should, for any self-respecting woman only happen within the sanctity of marriage.'

At the time, I had been confused, but I always remember the sadness of the girl's expression as she said, 'When the mighty fall, they fall.'

I could never have anticipated how very far I would fall from grace. My biggest sign of protest was yet to come, when I refused to travel from London to Scotland on a very cold day in 1960.

Chapter 3

Why the sadness?

Sam looks across the cafe at the smart, grey-haired woman, and thinks of his wife – Maria Anderson, nee Potter; a strong, independent woman through and through. Their journey to this stage had been a long painful process. Once they recovered from a very difficult and sad time in their marriage, she had supported him to go to college – a decision that had not been without its challenges, particularly with young children to care for. He remembers how guilty he used to feel leaving Maria, particularly when he was away on placement and could not return at night. But she had always assured him it was fine.

Even now, after so many years, Sam feels sad when he remembers how much his girls had missed him. Their eldest on one occasion, had begun to fret for him. When she cried that she wanted her daddy, Maria had reassured her he would be home in fourteen days.

'No,' their daughter had cried. 'No, no, no! You said he will be back in two weeks.'

He and Maria had chuckled over the story when she told him on his return, both of them gently amused at how innocent their girls were. He knew Maria had loved being a mother, even though it was particularly hard work when he was away.

His only consolation had been that he was determined to build a better future for her and their precious family.

Over the years, Sam had worked hard to secure jobs related to his training; having thrived and advanced, he had been able to ensure his family was financially secure. Sam had always been slightly more frivolous with money, while Maria was the more frugal one.

He looked around the café, taking in the bright surroundings, the cheerfulness of the décor. *How did we ever manage to save for this dream?* In his heart, he knows that it was Maria who had always remained focused on their dream.

They had decided years ago that one day they would open a café like no other; one which offered healthy food. *How topical,* he thinks, then smiles. *Or is it tropical?* He laughs aloud then looks quickly around to ensure no-one has seen him.

For a moment he is distracted from his thoughts, as he observes the body language of the woman again. Slightly slouched, she stares at her cup of tea then out of the window. She appears to sigh, sits back, rubs her face, then looks around, before settling back into the seat. He watches, fascinated, as she allows her shoulders to drop, making her appear more relaxed, more like the occupants of the other tables. The incessant chattering within the café is almost like the low hum of busy bees going about their business.

The woman's posture somehow touches a nerve in him; one he doesn't like exposing. It is too painful. It can still ache. It brings back too many memories of the heartache which he and Maria went through. How hard it had been. He recalls how they had naively talked of having a honeymoon baby. Yes, they had joked, nine months after their wedding, the first of their large family would arrive on cue.

But month after month, nothing happened. They were terrible times, trying unsuccessfully to conceive a baby. Then the feelings of failure followed, as they shared their tears each month, left empty with disappointment.

The haunted look on Maria's face would appear every month. For two or three days she would be elated, hopeful, convinced that this time she felt different. Then for two days after, she would eat nothing, just weeping like her heart was breaking. The sadness in her posture would greet him as he came home from work, finding her staring out of the window as though searching for a lost soul. Her spirit began to break a little more, with each passing, disappointing month. The pain in her heart grew worse with each passing month. The pretence to the outside world was so difficult to maintain.

They both tried to put on a brave face to family and friends, who continually asked, 'When will we hear the pitter-patter of tiny feet?'

There was always lightness in the tone of the voices of curious relatives and workmates. 'Thought you two were having a honeymoon baby?'

'Oh, not just at the moment,' either he or Maria would reply. But as the months went by, family visits became harder to bear as they tried to disguise their pain.

Sam sighs, picks up a tea towel, and absent-mindedly begins to dry glasses on the counter. Unless you've experienced it, no-one can understand how difficult it is for a couple desperate to conceive. Even the strongest and most loving relationship begins to get tested to the limit by not being able to produce the very thing which you perceive will make you both complete.

A few years of nothing was followed by an array of visits to doctors, that smell of hospital rooms can still stir negative feelings. Everything felt cold. Everything was clinical. The linoleum was made in the east coast, in a factory familiar to them both. It felt hard beneath their feet as they sat and waited for the current medical prognosis, which broke both their hearts a little more with each passing month.

'Come in, nice to see you, Mr. and Mrs. Anderson.' Sam remembers so clearly the doctor's greeting as he continued to make notes in the previous patient's file. 'Will be with you in a minute.'

Eventually, he had lifted his head and smiled – an insincere smile, Sam thought, sharing a glance with Maria. Why was this man showing an apparent lack of compassion towards something so very, very sensitive?

'Yes, nice to see you too, Doctor.' They had genuinely meant their reply, desperately clinging to the hope that this visit might just provide them with the answer to their problems.

When the doctor said, 'Please take a seat', Sam had looked at the red leather and wooden-framed chair. His nerves getting the better of him, jumbling thoughts of lifting the chair and taking it home to their living room. Managing to stifle his laughter, which would have been so inappropriate, he had pulled himself together and sat down, preparing to listen to what the doctor had to say.

What followed were many difficult hospital visits, which had produced nothing but sterile environments where the most intimate details of their personal life had been exposed. Probing personal questions, and examinations month after month, meetings to discuss any new treatment which might be of assistance. Have you tried this? Have you tried that? Have you tried the next thing? They had sat and listened to each medical professional, their eyes meeting with sadness as they shared similar thoughts at the patronising tones of this professor or that consultant.

They had felt so utterly helpless, so powerless, yet they knew they needed to endure all this intrusion into the most intimate part of their lives if they were to have even the slightest chance of conceiving that precious and long-awaited baby.

Chapter 4

Loss and grief

Sam had begun to struggle with Maria's deep unhappiness. They had drifted so far apart that they were on the point of breaking. He had been adamant that he did not want to adopt children. Why? Because it hurt to think he could not have one of his own.

Despite his feelings, Maria had still wanted to adopt, and it became a difficult issue for them to overcome due to their polar opposite opinions. Neither of them was willing to compromise so there was no give. The subject was spoken about, argued about, and eventually became their 'elephant' in the room; the longer the situation dragged on, the harder it became to try to resolve it.

'Sam, Sam,' she had pleaded. 'Can we please talk about this?'

Silence. Then Maria sighed louder and pointed to the physical gap between them.

'SAM!'

Startled, he had replied without making eye contact, 'What about?'

'You know very well.' Another sigh of exasperation. 'Never mind.'

'Maria, Maria, wait,' he'd replied wearily. 'I just think we've talked it to death. Why don't we just wait and see what happens?'

This time she had not raised her voice, but instead turned her head and he'd heard the muffled sounds of her crying as she looked out of the window.

Even now, Sam berates himself for not being any good at dealing with Maria's deep emotional pain at that time. He remembers his own pain of not being able to do anything. How many nights had they spent like that? So many evenings consumed by silence. So many times he'd thought, 'I just can't do this. I just can't do this.' He felt Maria never really understood the impact this defeat would have on how he was perceived by their friends and family, the people he knew at the cricket club.

He had lost count of how many nights this same scenario became such a big part of their lives, where they would not talk for the rest of the night. They would each retreat into their private worlds of silence and pain, leaving the atmosphere in the room full of sadness and regret. Maria had always been the first to admit defeat and go to bed. She would get up from where she was sitting, rearrange the cushions on the settee, then say in a clipped tone, 'Goodnight, Sam.'

'Goodnight Maria,' his reply was always cool.

But after she went upstairs, he would question himself so much, desperate to follow her, then realising he just couldn't face another battle.

Sam can still remember those nights so vividly. Maria would walk quietly up a few creaking stairs, then stop, and after a few minutes the creaking would start creek again. He knew her so well; he had known she was waiting and listening to see if Sam would follow. But he never did. It was all so different from the giggles and chatter of the early days of their marriage.

Downstairs, often sitting in the darkness, he would imagine her following her familiar routine. After going to the bathroom, she would quietly move to their bedroom. The room itself had been spacious in comparison to the other rooms in the house, particularly compared to the other bedroom which they had hoped would become the nursery.

She would walk over to the expensive G-plan dressing table, its honey-coloured wood complemented by the soft cream drawers. She'd lift the lid, after pulling out the stool which sat under it, and position herself where she had a maximum view of her face and trunk. No doubt finding comfort in her routine, she would then cleanse her face and neck, brush her hair, then finally rub moisturiser into her hands.

Even now, Sam can still see that bedroom in his mind. The cream curtains, with an embossed pattern in the exact same shade eloquently detailed across them, which blended beautifully with the other furnishings. Then there were the G-plan bedside cabinets to match the dressing table. The beautiful bedspread had taken Maria such a long time to find.

She'd move round the room, probably trying to alleviate her pain by admiring how their room was, in her opinion, just perfect: the feast of delicate trimmings on the bedspread, which draped like a dream onto the floor; the cream lace border round the outer edge, and a square strategically placed in the middle of the cover; the green sprig, along with the rose-coloured flower, so comforting to the eye.

Once changed into her nightclothes, she would go down on bended knees by the side of the bed to say her prayers, then climb into bed, switching off her bedside lamp to await a restful sleep, which rarely came.

Meanwhile, still downstairs, Sam had been tortured by his own thoughts: *Why can't we just have our own babies? It would make life so simple.*

Still polishing a glass, oblivious to the chatter in the café, he can't shake the memories of those evenings when he'd stay downstairs, trying to read his book, until the BBC shutdown music would start playing on the TV. The logo on the screen was a girl, a circle and squares, with an inane sound to remind viewers to turn the blasted thing off.

He would wearily rise from his seat, turn the TV off, and slowly head upstairs. Night after night, he had been restless. Maria had been the same, but neither of them had spoken, both locked in their own darkness; there was not even a chink of light from the window. The sound of breathing in the room had not been that of two people deep in peaceful slumbers. The silence was like a wall between them, with neither one prepared to climb over it to reach the other.

Maria had gone through so many different stages. At times, she had been angry. Other times, she showed such frustration, where she would shout at him for something as simple as not folding his newspaper and putting it in the magazine rack. Why? She had been convinced she was being rational, even though her tone of voice had been clipped.

Then she had become silent; he was convinced she was being stubborn and he would run. But he had still refused to give in. Deep down, he had understood that she was being pushed to the limit by her desire to be a mother, no matter what. As they began to argue and bicker almost constantly over small, unimportant issues, he had begun to realise that they were stuck while Maria still felt such a yearning to be a mother.

This emotional rollercoaster had gone faster and faster until it suddenly ground to a halt, and eventually they had both felt trapped in the depths of sadness that spilled over. The colourful and happy life they had anticipated and longed-for should by then have been completed by the arrival of their babies. Instead, cold stony silence was suffocating them.

When had sadness turned to bitterness, then to being embittered? Sam shivered now at the memory of those horrendous times. They had become so far apart and out of their depth that they'd had no idea how to get back to shore. *Did they even want to?*

Always a principled man, he had been convinced Maria would eventually see things his way. She usually did.

'Not this time, Sam,' she'd said.

Sam had become more and more frightened. She became quieter and quieter, till she had no fight left in her. Eventually, she had been unable to function on a day-to-day basis, spending each day sitting in her dressing gown, staring aimlessly at the four walls. She had looked at him with such sadness in her eyes.

The sound of silence, a sad lonely silence, filtered the house daily alongside the dust. Sam had never thought dust could smell, but he had learned that it does when someone is so unhappy, and cleaning is the last thing on the agenda when someone is nursing a broken heart. A previously immaculate woman, she would often sit unwashed, her tangled hair uncombed; it was not a pretty sight. He'd had no idea what to do. He had begun to forget what their life had been like before the much-anticipated honeymoon baby. *How did that happen? How would they ever recover?*

He sighed again, but with relief this time. They *had* survived.

One day, unexpectedly, Maria had said, 'Sam, you win.'

'What do you mean?'

'I can't keep going on like this,' she'd whispered.

His shoulders slumped. 'I know.' Her words had hit him harder than he could ever have imagined.

'What do you mean?' Maria had looked confused and so weary.

'I am a fool. I have been so stubborn.' The pain he had felt then still feels raw today. 'I am so sorry,' he'd told her, clasping her cold hands. 'I want us to have a family, so I will look at all the other options and speak to the doctor next time we are at the clinic. I don't want us to continue like this. I have been so sad and lonely.'

He shudders and physically shakes, like trying to remove a wet, heavy coat. Thankfully, it had proved to be the first step on their road to recovery – one which had taken a long, long time to achieve. But Sam knows in his heart that they finally gained a full life – every time he thinks of his children.

Chapter 5

Lost expectations

Sam is jolted back from his thoughts by a sudden unexplained noise. He shudders again as if to switch off the pain, and searches not so deeply into another part of his brain. He does a quick shift, almost like a dancer with complete precision. He feels the pain disperse as the flow of happiness gradually goes from his heart to his brain. His eyes shine. He thinks of the life he and Maria carved for themselves. A flat overlooking the sea, with the spectacular view once the haar lifted. Ah, such simple pleasures to follow a hard day in the office, a hot cuppa and your baffies – slippers, if you don't hail from the east coast – at the end of a hard day.

Then there had been a move away from their extended family when 'the job' came along. They had spoken at great length about this.

'What do you think?' Sam remembers asking, still unsure.

They knew they would both miss their families – their parents, brothers, sisters, nieces, nephews – and they would be living so far away.

'I promise we will definitely come back at least every Christmas,' Sam had assured her. 'Let's try it. We can always come home if it doesn't work out. Someone in the family will put us up till we get a house again.'

'Ok, but you promise every Christmas?' Maria had asked.

'Yes,' he'd replied, hugging her.

They had both known it would be a good opportunity for a fresh start, despite their parents' sadness at seeing them move away. Within a couple of months, they had packed up, said their goodbyes, and moved.

At times it had been hard for them both; they missed the big get-togethers with both families, their siblings, and their offspring. *That makes them sound like burst pipes!* Sam has a chuckle at another of his made-up jokes.

But over the next few years, along had come the family affectionately referred to as 'the girls'. Sam can't help but smile broadly. *They will always be my girls, although they are all grown up with families of their own; our grandchildren. How quickly the years have gone.*

Focusing back on his current surroundings, Sam looks over at the woman at the corner table by the window. How sad she looks today.

He is vaguely aware that she seems to stay for longer than normal today. Usually throughout the year, she comes in and has her tea – it always has to be Ceylonese – then leaves. But today, she has been in, gone out, and come back several times throughout the day.

She seems to be gazing across the road to where the homeless hostel building used to sit. *Or is she looking beyond that? Who would know?*

***

Nadia is deep in thought as she sips her tea. How can things be so very different now?

She is distracted from her musings as she watches a young mum struggling to manoeuvre a pram across the busy road. *Where has the girl come from? Where is she going in such a hurry? She looks so out of place with her pram in this busy area of London. Is her story as sad as mine? Is she happy? How times have changed. Would she even know how sad it was for women like me when I was her age?*

The woman is certainly privileged enough to have had her baby in a time when it is socially and, for some, culturally acceptable to have babies, regardless of your marital status. There is support for women much more than there was when she was young. At that time, the institution of marriage was sacrosanct.

It was then, and only then, that you could consider procreation. Well, that's what the church taught her.

Aren't babies created in all different circumstances? she questions. Not in the eyes of the church. Their perspective at that time was the 'Gospel according to…'. Babies should only be created within the boundaries of a marriage.

Did all religions believe that? Or just hers? God is everywhere, she remembers being taught.

Did He see my atrocity? If he did, why did He not stop me? How stupid was I?

The unspoken crime of her religion was that to be pregnant outside marriage was an atrocity of the highest degree. In the 1960s, if you found out you were pregnant, some women were able to be married off; 'shotgun' weddings was the expression used at that time to force the man to take responsibility for his actions. This was not the case for Nadia. Instead, the man had been banished never to return.

Her mind is a whirl of questions: *Once you had your baby, you made the decision. That is a joke in itself. How many women were forced to make this decision? Who decides to become pregnant, have a baby, then give their baby up for adoption? But what other choices were available? When you were told to leave and not come back till you had got rid of the 'bastard' child, there was no way back to your baby, even if you immediately regretted this decision.*

The baby was supposed to spend six weeks with the mother, before the legal consent form for adoption could be signed by her. After that, it was final. How could anyone understand what that feels like? No-one can. Nadia's baby had been about to be taken from her before the six weeks, and yet no-one cared. *I was frightened. I tried so very hard to keep my baby, to no avail.*

She blinks back tears. *How was it allowed to happen? Did they care? It would appear not. I was incarcerated in a 'mother and baby home'. Why? I am heartbroken, and no-one cares. I was just another 'unruly' woman who had got herself into 'trouble'.*

Why did they do it to her? She has never properly understood. Her parents could easily have accommodated her baby into their loving family and pretended to society that it was a relative's baby coming to live with us. The excuse would have been unimportant. Her sister-in-law could have pretended to be the mother, who was unable to look after the child. Or Nadia's cousin, who was also in London. It was common practice in those days time to abate any suspicion that the baby had been conceived out of wedlock. Yet no such luxury was bestowed on Nadia from the highest power down. The church, the family, and society were more powerful than any rebellious acts she could ever have conjured up.

That fateful day, after weeks of waiting, came to Nadia as it did to every other girl in the 'mother and baby home'. She sips her tea, barely tasting the hot liquid as she remembers. She had always thought the word 'home' meant a comfortable place, to feel safe and secure. But not there. She had soon found out the opposite was true. It turned out to be a place of terror, torture, pain, and extreme heartbreak which was to last a lifetime. Long after her baby had gone.

When she had first arrived there, she had kept rubbing her tummy, hoping to connect with her baby. All the girls were expected to work hard during the day to earn their keep; in Nadia's case, she was assigned to laundry duties. There had been a great camaraderie within the workplace, with all the young girls rallying together to support each other. But no matter how 'brave' they tried to be in daytime, at night the heaviness in the air of grief, loss, and pain was suffocating.

Then her turn had come. The searing pain reminded her of the sadness which affected her as she wept each night, feeling so alone and unloved. She often heard the stifled sobs of others crying into their pillows once the lights went out. She was sure it had been the same for each and every one of them.

Nadia's fateful day started on the 14th November. She remembers standing beside the boiler, pulling out the sheets, when she felt the pain start. It was a niggle at first and then, as the hours passed it, became more intense.

But still she kept working. She knew she had to pay for her 'sins'.

She had worked and worked, but the pain was building. Yet she kept telling herself that she had to endure whatever awaited her, for God was not happy with her.

Her friend of a few weeks – Monica – went over to the nun on duty.

'Sister, you need to come and help my friend.'

'What?'

'Sister, you need to come and help my friend. Her baby is coming.'

'Yes, alright. I will deal with this. Back to work.'

As the nun approached her, Nadia had smiled at her friend as a thank you for her help. The nun then took her by the arm, but her touch was cold and clinical, ensuring she remained emotionally detached at all times from the 'sinner'.

Directed to 'the room', Nadia began to feel very frightened and so very, very alone.

Once there, she was told to put a white gown on. She did as instructed, and waited. The nun examined her, but when Nadia rubbed her tummy, the nun told her to stop doing that. She did as she was told, but could not prevent herself from thinking: *If she is 'married' to God, he must be a horrible man if she is so mean.*

The pain came. The pain went. That was the pattern for a very long time. The doctor was called when it was about time. *They must do this often*, Nadia thought, because he came into the room and very soon after, little Mafalda was born in the late hours of the 15th November.

Nadia was allowed to look at her baby. She was beautiful. She looked a lot like Ralf, Nadia's brother. But in many ways, it was like looking in a mirror; Nadia saw so much of herself in this tiny, perfect little face as the baby snuggled into her like they were one. She knew little Mafalda was going to have to be a powerful battler to survive.

Not a trace of her atrocity with Mansui was to be seen. How was this possible? Had God forgiven her? Nadia began to feel a little bit hopeful; maybe they would let her keep her child. But her hopes were in vain, as she was about to find out a few weeks later.

All of the children born in that 'baby factory' were born out of wedlock. For many, the shame from society would live on in their hearts. It certainly did for Nadia; it remained with her every day.

Nadia sighs again as she remembers those early days of her child's life. She has carved out a life for herself – and life goes on. But she will never understand or comprehend why society shunned her and those other women in her position. In her case, it was to prevent shame on her family; yes, shame.

But no-one will ever convince her that her baby, like so many others, could not have become part of her wider family.

In the first weeks after Mafalda's birth, she wished that her brother and his wife could forgive her, to let her return home and pretend that the baby was theirs and they were unable to look after her until they were settled. Perhaps one of her cousins would know that this baby was not responsible for her sins, and take pity on her, to allow her to keep her beautiful little daughter.

She was less hopeful of Ralf and his wife changing their mind, given their disapproval at her attempts at a pointless protest. But what else could she have done?

The acute pain of being forced, against your will, to give your baby up for adoption is timeless. Nadia knew she was not alone in this pain; she feels the pain daily. Many women her age feel it too she is sure. She briefly remembers feeling so sad when not so long ago she read an article in a newspaper about an elderly woman who had died, and skeletons of babies were found in her attic.

Why? Why? Why?

Nadia shakes away her memories and looks around the café again, wondering about the circumstances of the young women in the room. Is *she* married? That girl; is she 'living in sin', as it was called when Nadia was young? Is that woman in the corner married and divorced, and in a new blended relationship? Would she comprehend Nadia's experience in its entirety? She thinks not; it's doubtful any of them would ever be forced to go through what she went through.

She bites her lip to hold back hot tears, as her thoughts take over again. *And where is my baby? What happened to her?*

Chapter 6

Sunshine for Nadia

Twenty-first century Ceylon: how has it changed since I was last there?

The country was renamed Sri Lanka, but I wonder how much else has changed. Even now, sitting in a London café on a wet late summer evening, I can almost feel the sun beating down on my back. It was always so warm, and my body starts to relax with the memory of how wonderful it felt.

Another thought makes me re member fondly the smell of Dahl cooking. The aroma of the cumin, coriander, and garam masala almost makes my mouth water as I remember the wonderful dahl we had on so many sunny nights back home. The air of happiness in people's voices for some reason was lifted by the warm Ceylonese weather in summer. Oh, you have to experience first-hand the bold and bright colours associated with my country, they are even more spectacular than any holiday brochure photographs. The strong, vibrant yellow – like sunshine. The bold red – like a striking pepper. The intense pink of a beautiful Japanese azalea bush in full bloom. The magnificent turquoise blue, which always reminded me of the cool ocean. These stimulated my senses for so long, and were so familiar to me for my entire childhood.

I'd thought they were gone forever, but it's strange how you can never forget certain memories. And even today, I can still close my eyes and breathe in those amazing smells, and hear the sounds of all the people coming and going, and the wonderful echo of their feet on the dry, dusty streets.

Where are they all going? What are they all doing? Where am I? I allow my mind to wander, and the memories are still so vivid after all these years. How I loved sitting outside that café in Ceylon, watching the world go by.

Those memories of so very long ago can still fill my senses, if I allow myself to indulge in them. They still provide me with a familiar comfort which I enjoyed back then. Ceylon held a special place in my heart... before my atrocity.

What happened to Ceylon? She was lost forever in 1972, when she became Sri Lanka. This beautiful island, situated in the Indian Ocean, is renowned worldwide for its high-quality tea. In fact, it's the third biggest tea producing country in the world. But it trades other valuable commodities such as coconut and rubber, along with an abundance of pepper and spices ripened to perfection. Its history dates back to 1736, when it was one of the Commonwealth countries. How many people also know that there is a strong Portuguese influence there?

The people have a strong sense of spirituality – as meditation forms a large part of many of their lives. And holidaymakers to the island often seek a deeper understanding of the philosophy behind the spiritual aspect of meditation. 'Buddhism is the limelight of Sri Lankan Civilization from ancient times.' Everything about Sri Lankan life is related to Buddhism, but there it is called Theravada – the main focus being to give priority to the philosophy of living a simple life.

In the 21st century, however, Sri Lanka appears to be a country of diversity. How is this possible? Doesn't her history define her today as it did when she was Ceylon?

I used to sit in that café long ago, watching people come and go from the centre of the business capital where there appeared to be an illusion of complete opulence. The new world trade centre of Colombo was sited nearby, in a 40-storey twin tower complex – one of the most modern exchanges in South Asia. Growing up, I had often visited the old parliament building and ancient churches, even ridden in a tuk-tuk, which was great fun and an efficient way to get around the city.

Some years ago, in a moment of weakness, I went back for a holiday. How did I ever succumb? I went into a travel agency and, before I knew it, the young girl behind the desk was enthusiastically telling me she was getting married and going on honeymoon to Maldives and then Sri Lanka, for the holiday of a lifetime. As we chatted, her enthusiasm sparked something within me, and I had booked the trip to Sri Lanka before I left the shop.

I was finally going back.

In the run-up to the trip, I felt a real sense of trepidation, given my extradition. The travel agent's enthusiasm began to wane, and my anxieties stayed with me throughout my visit.

I remember sitting outside a café in Colombo, wondering and hoping that the country had changed for the better. A couple nearby caught my attention. 'Honey, over here!' the man waved his hand to get the attention of someone across the street.

As the woman approached, smiling, he said, 'Look, these are beautiful, don't you agree? The cotton feels delightful, what do you think?' He touched the fabric.

I remember them so clearly. The woman reached into a bag and pulled out a vibrant yellow and deep purple and pink sarong. She had just come from Laskala at Fort – a store boasting an abundance of handicrafts produced all over the island.

Seeing the young couple so happy and enjoying my culture, a sad longing had washed over me despite the sunshine. What if things could have been different?

It wasn't the young couple I resented, just the fact that Sri Lanka welcomed them when Ceylon had rejected me.

They looked just as I had felt so very long ago – young and alive, with an obvious ease to their relationship, something I had then but lost forever. How many young people are so caught up in their own excitement that they look at older people and never see beyond the grey hair, the thickened waists and slower bodies?

The Ceylon I remember is not the Sri Lanka of today. It brought me no comfort.

After I returned from my trip, the months of that year passed so quickly... until once again it was the 15th November.

Chapter 7

Why me? Why not me?

I have come back to the only place where I find comfort at this time of year. The Cinnamon Café.

I ask for my bill, leave the café, and walk out onto the busy London street then make my way home by my usual route. When I eventually arrive there, I take off my coat and immediately run myself a hot bath with my favourite aromatic essences to soothe my aching body. I have done this on so many occasions, but today is the 15th November, and on this date nothing provides me with any sense of comfort or prevents the feelings associated with the loss of my baby so very long ago.

Those feelings ebb and flow through my veins like the tide, providing some sense of familiarity over the last 40 years. Every November, they feel like putting on an old, weather-beaten, wet, woollen, heavy tweed coat, with enormous buttons that are so difficult to do up that they are left undone, exposing my vulnerable heart to the winter elements.

Over 40 years now, I remind myself, as I wander round my meticulously organised and clean flat. When I was young, I used to love kicking off my shoes and leaving them in my room, where they lay till the morning. Those carefree days are long gone.

My heart tells me I should have carved a better life for myself by leaving the past behind. I shudder when I remember the shame on my mother's face when my efforts to conceal the changes to my young, round body, began to fail. I remember that day as clearly as if it were yesterday. Until then, I had managed to feign normality every month, praying that once my atrocity was revealed, it could remain a secret within the family.

My brain retrieves the memory. How familiar yet so very far away, the smell of the dry, warm weather, the sound of the gentle breeze flowing through the trees, the love and emotional support from within my family. How lucky I felt. Especially, looking back, the special bond I shared with my brother Ralf. I loved him with all my heart and would have trusted him with my life. He always called me 'little one' – an affectionate name which I cherished as a young girl.

I remember how he patiently accepted that I liked to wander and observe the natural beauty en route to school, after we were dropped at the secure gates, before going inside the building.

I still feel so hurt that he deserted me in my time of need. He always appeared to understand me completely, yet he left me. *I thought you would help me Ralf, but you betrayed me when I needed you most, and 'little one' was lost forever. Why?*

I try to shake the memories away, but they keep coming back. My mother was such an elegant woman, slim-built, her petite, cinnamon features enhanced by large, dark eyes. Was she beautiful? To me, yes. She certainly exuded an air of quiet confidence.

That fateful day, I stood in the doorway, observing my mother making herself a cup of tea. I remember drinking in the vision before me. At that moment in time, I was so sure she was blissfully unaware of my situation.

Mother stood still, continuing to stir the tea, then stopped. Looking up at me, she asked if there was something she should know about me.

'What do you mean?' I asked innocently.

'I have noticed you are different, Nadia.'

'What have you noticed?' I spluttered, trying to appear controlled.

'You know.'

I would never challenge my mother. At that point, I realised with a sinking heart that she knew.

Chapter 8

Can history repeat itself?

I am very restless, and wonder if my recent trip caused these feelings to resurface. Was I a foolish old woman to go back there, and allow even a chink of light into my darkened heart? I had so successfully compartmentalised that part of my life up until now.

As I slide into the warm bath water to soak away the pain of the day, my mind starts to wander and once again I wonder why my country of origin still means so much to me. Why had its history always fascinated me, before my unjustifiable fall from grace? Perhaps it was because of the powerful woman who rose to lead the country in such tragic circumstances.

The Ceylon of my time was so very traditional. Was I so naïve, or plain stupid, to think I could be like her? I kept hoping against hope that my parents would remember how excited I had been to think how forward-thinking the country was in electing the first woman prime minister – Sirimavo Bandaranaike, widow of the assassinated prime minister.

The Roman Catholic Church's influence was such an overt part of Ceylon's culture, as many high caste families were educated by nuns. Mrs Bandaranaike was an aristocrat by birth – born into the Ceylon aristocracy – and her husband was a landowner. She was educated by Roman Catholic nuns in the capital, Colombo, as well as being a practising Buddhist. Married in 1940, aged 24, she and her husband had three children and she seemed content in her role as mother and wife until his death. Then she became well known as the 'weeping widow', frequently bursting into tears during the election campaign as she vowed to continue her late husband's socialist policies.

Why then did my country of origin make history by accepting a woman as head of state, yet reject and banish me simply for being a woman?

Mrs Bandaranaike's mother-in-law was another strong woman within a society dominated by men. Daisy Obeyesekere, who revolted against tradition by leaving her husband and living an independent life in Colombo, became the first president of the Women's Franchise Union, and an important influence on her son.

High caste families had – and still have – more choices than many, due to their powerful influence within and outwith the community. Looking at these powerful role models, I had naively begun to believe that I might have a choice about my pregnancy. Maybe my parents would understand and let me live a life like Daisy Obeyesekere. I could work and support my child, I could move to another area where no-one would know me; I had choices, didn't I?

But the more I deliberated, the more afraid I became. Who would understand? What was I going to do? I tried to convince myself that the whole sorry situation would be worked out by my loving family. What I wasn't prepared for was that my whole world would change forever.

I was given no choice. Being part of a deeply religious family where sex before marriage was a sin, where an illegitimate baby was a symbol of this 'sin,' where the power of the Church was feared by all parishioners, it was made clear to me: my baby was going to be illegitimate, and my family would not tolerate this.

Chapter 9

What choice?

Lying soaking in the bath, I torture myself over what happened to my child. Did she carry a romantic notion that perhaps I had been too poor to look after her? Certainly, anyone who could afford a passage from Britain to Ceylon at that time, was indeed financially secure.

Did my child think I paid to remove all traces of her? She would be so wrong. I knew from others that to remove all traces of my atrocity, money would be donated to the mother and baby home to pay for my lodgings and to keep the baby until it was adopted. My family – not me – wanted to remove all traces of my little Mafalda.

Despite my pleading, they managed to do just that. But it was 1960s Britain not 21st century Britain. The decisions were taken out of my hands as I had brought shame on my family. I was not to know at that point that things would never be the same for me again.

On days like this, I can so easily recall memories of that unborn life growing within me, despite all my efforts to bury those thoughts deep in my subconscious. How is it possible? I have worked so hard over the years trying to erase that time in my life, to put the past behind me, to move on. But it will not go. It is always there. It hurts. It's so painful.

My letter. Oh, my letter; I know every word within it. Miss K, the social worker, was so kind to me, assuring me she would keep my letter safe so Mafalda could have it if she ever came to the adoption society to find any traces of me. Before we were parted, I used to whisper in little Mafalda's ear, 'Always remember you are my powerful battler, and one day we will meet again.'

I really believed Miss K, but with each passing year, the flicker of hope is dying that we will ever meet again. I have thought on so many occasions that perhaps I should try to find Mafalda myself. But I know I am not worthy. I can only hope my Mafalda knows I had no choice.

I can quote my letter verbatim, even after all these years. My heart was breaking as I wrote it, as I wanted so much to keep my little Mafalda. She was mine, not theirs to steal.

Dear Miss K, I wrote.

I received your letter in hospital. Sorry for the delay in replying. I was terribly upset about parting with the baby. I was compelled to give the child on the 28th to the adoption officer. She was taken to the home, which is very pathetic to think of. When I think of this I keep crying, with nothing to be done. The nuns too did not like my keeping the child. They wanted me to do this and go back to my mother.

Since I am not allowed home, I wanted to keep her because I am responsible for bringing her into the world. I should never have had this baby. Poor thing, she has to go through any treatment given to her for my sins. I can never get over this. I keep praying. My mother wants me home, so I cannot work and have her. It is heart-breaking to think that she won't have anybody of her own in this country. What do you think of the home where coloured children are kept?

Thanks very much for the prayers you offered me. I had a diffi-cult time but never got over everything by the help of prayers. I had

her on the 15th of this month and away in two weeks, which is
heart-breaking. We are not used to giving away babies. This is the
first time a thing like this happened in our family. My own sins have
given me so much trouble.
Yours sincerely,
Nadia

It makes me so sad to remember this. Why was this time in history so hard for so many women who found themselves in similar situations? The situation was clearly dictated to by that time in the society I was part of. But was my family's social standing more important than my baby? It would appear so. Should I not have perhaps had more choices? It would appear not. My crime against society was to be unwed and pregnant. Irrespective of the circumstances, women of my generation were all powerless, before and after.

My parents could have let me keep my baby. We could have given her a life as part of our family. We were a faith-based, loving family. Yes, we were. I know we were.

When she was taken away, I tortured myself with all sorts of questions. What would become of my baby? She must be bought up in a certain faith. She must not be left alone. She must be adopted.

But how realistic was this for my baby in 1960? The reality was that fewer children were adopted by couples if they were not Caucasian. How would they find someone ethnically compatible with my little Mafalda, in a nearly all-white Britain?

My heart felt like it was breaking, even though Miss K did her utmost to convince me to the contrary. 'Nadia, listen to me very carefully,' the social worker said. 'The adoption societies do try to match the child to the parents. We make every effort to make the family compatible, to be able to present a family unit which is blended. This means that no-one ever needs to know the baby is not biologically theirs.

'That way, it is nice and easy to give the new parents the choice of telling the child they are adopted or not in some cases.'

'Will this be the same for my baby?' I asked.

'We will just have to wait and see.'

Throughout those terrible weeks, I believed Ralf would help me. But our bond was stretched and stretched until it was horribly snapped and broken.

I understood that it was not uncommon for unwed mothers and babies to be separated in the 1960s. In devoutly religious Ireland, many girls were sent to workhouses, like I was, until their babies were born. Like me, they had all choice removed, due to their ultimate sin – having an illegitimate child. Where did *their* babies go?

I had been part of a high caste family in Ceylon, which had strong connections with the church. When I was sent to Britain, the nuns were responsible for securing a place for me in a mother and baby home. Why the nuns? When did Ceylon become a Catholic country? And was there any relationship between religion and power?

I know in my heart that the influence of the church, its relationship with the governments at that time in both Britain and Ceylon, as well as the high caste system, all appear to have been interlinked. Because, in their eyes, I had 'sinned', I was powerless over how this influence was to impact on me.

Enough, Nadia, enough. I know I cannot turn back time, but how I wish I had been stronger at the time. Yet it is impossible and unrealistic to believe I could have changed the course of my destiny.

It is now the 21st century, and I must remind myself how much things have changed. Those young women I have seen when I visit the Cinnamon Café are so lucky to have the luxury of choices which women like me were denied.

I get out of my bath, dry myself, and wrap myself in the comfort of my cosy bath robe, before making my way through to my sitting room. I am still restless. The bath has not soothed my emotional pain. I consider pouring myself a large drink, in the hope it may help... but reconsider. Instead, I search for my other 'guilty pleasure' and settle for a very large packet of crisps and one small Bacardi and Coke to wash them down.

As another emotional November 15 comes to a close, I am grateful that I can tuck the date away in my heart for another year. Life goes on. It must, I know. Yet I find it difficult to accept that the older I become, the stronger is my yearning for answers about what happened to my baby. I know the law has changed and I could search for her, rather than wait for her to look for me. But I still don't feel worthy enough to take that step; if I'm honest, I have never overcome the shame of that terrible 'sin' all those years ago.

Chapter 10

Overcoming dark times

It's the 16th November, and Sam heads home after another busy day at the Cinnamon Café. Over a relaxing cup of tea, he and Maria take the chance to chat about the business and, as always, begin to reminisce. Although they are happy with their lives here, they both miss Scotland.

Maria looks affectionately at her husband. They have come through so much over the years, particularly her 'dark' time and the battle which raged between them for so long. 'How lucky we are. Thank God we made it.'

Sam smiles. 'When you were very ill, I realised that life is so precious and that every opportunity should be taken. That's the reason we are sitting here now, many miles from "home", but living our dream.'

She settles happily back into the comfortable settee, which they bought not long after their move south, and can't help but smile when she remembers the young salesman who sold them the three-piece suite all those years ago.

'The high-quality furniture represents a true investment in your home,' he'd told them enthusiastically. 'The armchair and both sofas would feature elegantly in any living room, with scroll-fronted arms, a sturdy hardwood frame, and sumptuous cushions.'

'Did you say scrumptious?' Sam had chortled, with his usual sense of humour. 'We don't plan to eat it, I want to sit on it.'

'No, sir. I said sumptuous,' the young man had corrected him.

She remembers so clearly how she had glowered at Sam to tell him to be quiet. The young man was obviously using a sales pitch which the manager must have outlined at the weekly staff meeting. Perhaps he should have told the young man to breathe and try to look more relaxed.

'The cushions are padded to offer long lasting comfort,' he'd continued, 'and its material is sturdy and easy to keep clean.'

After the long sales pitch, the young man had moved away – not too far away, but far enough. Probably directed by his manager, 'To give the customers time to ponder – not too long, though, or you may miss the sale.' When they told him they would take it, the boy had beamed with satisfaction at securing the deal.

At the time, it had seemed such an impulsive buy. But it still sits beautifully in their living room, with the two evergreen cushions and two fuchsia pink ones contrasting beautifully. Colour co-ordination has always been important and relaxing for Maria.

In contrast, some of the other furniture is beginning to look a bit jaded, but as a make-and-mend queen she will exhaust all other avenues before things will be replaced. After all, they were brought up in the war years. Her eyes are drawn to the photographs of the family and the grandchildren. *Such braw bairns*, she thinks, almost hugging herself in delight before musing: *We must update these the next time we are all together.*

She takes another sip of tea and thinks how lucky she is to have met Sam. Not all women have been so lucky. As she catches his eye, he smiles back at her.

'A penny for your thoughts.'

'Oh, just enjoying the moment,' she replies.

They both sit back quietly and enjoy the relaxing silence, before Maria speaks again. 'Can you imagine how different our lives would have been if you had passed your eleven-plus?'

'Indeed.' He nods. 'It was so hard at the time. Thank goodness our girls didn't have to go through that to qualify to continue in education. It wasn't so much failing the exam, it was the fact that the results determined which secondary school you were then eligible to attend, and often your future role in society.'

At that time, there were simple choices within the Scottish education system. You either left school at 14 to work or if you passed the 11 plus you could go on to further or higher education to become a tradesman, teacher or doctor. This then allowed young people the opportunity to qualify for professional jobs like teachers or doctors.

When Sam left school, he worked for a local greengrocer's shop, before going off to do his compulsory National Service in the Air Force. 'We could have conscripted or opt to go down the pits and become one of the Bevin Boys,' he recalls. 'But we were able to return to Civvie Street after the war, while many of my friends continued to work down the pits long after that.'

His life had turned out to be so different from his friend, Bob, who was a few years older than him. Bob had always felt aggrieved that he did his bit for the war movement by being a miner, yet received little or no recognition because they wore no uniforms unlike the services. 'It was so unfair on them,' Sam admits, sipping his tea, 'particularly as at that time there was a shortage of coal, so miners and their skills were necessary. Bob always called himself a "forgotten conscript". He got so fed up feeling like a second-class citizen that he went back and retrained as a mature student to become a teacher.'

Sam had enjoyed his time in the Air Force, and had secured a job as a clerk in a large company when he returned to Civvy Street. Not many people were earning £665 a year back then.

He thinks fondly of those earlier years of his life – meeting and courting Maria, their wedding, and those carefree days when he played football and cricket at weekends.

Maria, sitting across from him, recalls their early married years when she worked in the design room of a carpet factory – a job she had really loved, given her creative flair.

Their life had felt simple yet fulfilled. Moving into a flat with a sea view, which they loved, enjoying time together when they came home from work. Only one thing had marred this almost perfect life – their desperation to have a baby.

Chapter 11

Decisions

Sam yawns and puts his cup down on the small coffee table by the armchair. After a busy day, he is tired and heads on up to bed.

Sitting quietly in the sitting room, Maria's mind plays back over those early years and the difficult times they faced until they eventually decided to adopt. *And what a wonderful decision that was*, she thinks with a gentle smile. Their life had moved on through the years with all the trials and tribulations of family life. Then, with the girls grown and moving on with their own lives, she and Sam had made a life-changing decision to retire to London to pursue their dream of owning a café.

She sighs and closes her eyes briefly. It had been difficult at first, and she still found the unfamiliar sounds from the house a bit startling, but they had done it.

A noise outside disturbs Maria; it sounds like a baby crying. *Probably the alley cats at the back of the café fighting.* She hates that sound; it makes the hairs on the back of her neck stand on end. She has never liked cats, and would never consider going outside to chase them away. But she can rationalise her fear by accepting that it is less terrifying listening to this when she is indoors, and the noise passes much more quickly tonight. She realises she is holding her breath, and takes another sip of her tea as she gradually begins to relax again.

Maria's mind wanders back to the time when Sam decided to go to college. They had been a good team, and she had fallen in with society norm at that time as the homemaker while he was the breadwinner. Once Sam re-trained, he had worked full time and they saved for their ultimate dream of opening a café one day.

The funds grew, then were constantly depleted with the ongoing and often unexpected expenses of bringing up a family on one wage. But Maria smiles in satisfaction that they had finally achieved that dream. She knows so many people who made plans about what they would do when their children 'flew the nest', yet whose plans remained a pipedream – never a reality.

We made sure we tried it, and it's been the adventure of a lifetime. We may be in our seventies, but at least we can say we fulfilled our dream, she thinks contentedly.

Yet it could have been so very different, if Sam had passed that eleven-plus exam at school. *Where would we have been now?* she wonders.

Her husband's path had not been easy. He had struggled with failing the exam and it had a profound impact on him, especially as some of his family had done well and gone on to further education. Yet, in spite of his path taking a different route, she was proud of him and what he had since achieved.

She is well aware that he is not a man who likes to talk about emotional issues. But he has strength of character which has always been evident when they have faced major emotional issues. She thinks of the many times he has shown a soft, sensitive approach to supporting their girls through various crises in their lives.

Glimpses of family holidays, when the children were young, flash through her mind. Sam driving them on trips to the seaside; the girls and their friends playing in the sunshine and jumping in and out of the water from rope swings.

Their eldest, Zoe, had been frightened of the water, and it was Sam who had taught her how to swim.

'Dad, promise you won't let me go?'

'I promise.'

'Hold me, hold me.'

'I've got you, I won't let you go. Kick your feet and move your arms.'

'Ok.'

The terror on her daughter's face always twanged on Maria's heartstrings. Yet she did go on to learn to swim. With Sam's encouragement, Zoe went from dipping her feet at the edge of the pool until eventually being able to swim across the pool.

Sam had taught their girls the important things in life: helping others; to be non-judgmental about others less fortunate; to respect one another, even if they did not always agree.

Maria smiled to herself. With four growing girls, there had always been disagreements in the house. When they were young, the arguments were over toys, and as the girls got older there was the usual sibling rivalry over one thing or another – possibly heightened at times with hormonal imbalance, which could be loudly heard by all and sundry. In an effort to calm the situation, Maria would tell the culprits to 'turn the volume down', while Sam struggled as the only man in the house with five females.

'That's your sister,' he would be heard saying softly and calmly, to whichever of his daughters was shouting at the time.

'I hate her. Tell her...'

He'd look confused. 'Tell her what?'

'Oh,' was the disgusted reply. 'Never mind, you always stick up for her.'

The puzzled look on his face was often perceived as favour-itism, but he usually decided that it was not worth the energy trying to defend himself when the accuser was so clearly emotionally-charged. The angry daughter would then stomp off, complaining loudly that she was always the one being picked on while the others got away with it – whatever 'it' was at the time.

But there had also been plenty of laughter over the years. Sam had taught them to enjoy laughter and jokes, even if they did not find his jokes particularly funny. Maria slowly gets up from her chair and heads off to bed. Yes, she thinks, Sam is a good man.

***

The following evening, after work, Sam and Maria are relax-ing, catching up with the day's news on TV.

'Would you like a coffee?' Sam stands up and makes his way towards the kitchen.

'Yes, please.' Maria wraps her blue cashmere cardigan round her and hugs herself. She looks around the room and wonders: *Where have the years gone?* When the girls were young, sometimes the days seemed so long; but as her daughters got older, the nights seemed longer, as she worried about them going out into the world to carve their way, accepting the good and bad choices young adults make.

Maria has always been a firm believer that young people need to make their mistakes, to allow them to – hopefully – learn about the next stage in the adventure of life.

Her thoughts wander again, and she thinks about how their path could have been so very different, had she and Sam not decided on adoption.

She snaps back to reality as Sam comes back, coffee in hand, munching on something. *My favourite chocolate?* she wonders. *I have been trying to make that last.*

Her guess is confirmed when he hands Maria one square of her favourite chocolate. For a brief moment, she feels slightly annoyed that he has eaten his own and now he's helping to eat her bar. How frustrating it is to live with someone who can demolish a whole bar of chocolate in one sitting, while she prefers to savour just one square a day.

She realises that no matter how old you get, the things which annoy you in any relationship can still affect your mood. But when she looks across at him, she sees Sam smile and all her anger disperses. It's obvious that he knows what she has been thinking.

'I promise I'll buy you more tomorrow,' he assures her.

That is one thing, she thinks, that she does like about getting older. Such daft incidents don't really matter. She wouldn't change her life for anything.

Chapter 12

Contented family life

Sam loves breakfast time. *My favourite meal of the day*, he tells himself, as he sits down at the kitchen table. *Who are you kidding?* he smiles to himself. *I love all my meals; in fact, I just love food.*

As he tucks into his toast and poached eggs, he wonders where his enjoyment of food comes from. Perhaps it is linked to having lived through the rationing of food during the war. He distinctly remembers how the family's ration book was stamped every time they bought anything, and no-one was allowed to exceed their weekly quota of food. But he remembers fondly how some people would swap tokens with another family they were friendly with. Sometimes, mothers would start chatting while they were in the queue waiting to be served, and discover that another family did not like something, so they would swap. Ultimately, it meant his family gained extra portions of their favourite foods.

He shakes his head in amazement at how his mother managed to feed them all. There was no choice but to accept rationing during the war years, and there was certainly not the abundance of food there is now. Young people nowadays take so much for granted.

He mutters to himself. 'Maybe that's why Maria will have just one square of chocolate a day. But one square doesn't even tickle my taste buds.' He laughs out loud.

'What's so funny?' asks Maria, as she comes into the kitchen. 'Do these trousers not fit me? Does my bum look big in them?' Her brow wrinkles with concern. 'I bought them last week when I was up north.'

'No, they really suit you,' he assures her, and watches her affectionately as she follows her usual morning routine with precision.

Maria has always needed reassurance, a need to do things properly. He remembers when their eldest daughter had come to them, his wife would say, 'Oh Sam, we've never done this before. She is the experiment. What if we can't do it to perfection?'

'Perfection is boring, Maria,' he would reply. 'How will we ever learn if we don't make mistakes?' And he would watch her breathe a sigh of relief, then carry on with changing the baby's nappy, or feeding her, or comforting her.

He remembers how hard it was back then, particularly for Maria. When you adopted a child, the health visitor would visit and form an instant perception of your suitability to adopt a baby or child. Social Services looked at the baby to decide the suitability of the impending adoption, and whether the tot was best matched to the couple. They looked at your house, adding their own professional perspective of whether it was clean enough for a baby to come into. If a negative report was submitted relating to the home environment, then the child would not be released for adoption.

Maria had always been petrified this would be the case. Even though she had already cleaned the house from top to bottom, she would take a duster around again five minutes prior to that knock on the door which never failed to startle her. At every visit, she presented a cool and calm demeanour, which totally belied the emotional turmoil she was experiencing. And as soon as the social workers left, she would collapse on the settee, completely exhausted after trying to second-guess every question, desperate to provide what she hoped was a first-class response. On one occasion, he remembers, she was so tense that she blurted out, 'Well, do I get a gold star?' But her attempt at humour had been met with a look of complete disdain.

She hated the power game which was going on, but she knew they could do nothing about it; any complaint would be her word against the authorities, and she knew all too well who would win. She could not risk it.

Some evenings, after a social work visit, Sam would return from work to find Maria curled up on the settee, fast asleep in the foetal position. The first time it happened, he had held his breath anxiously as he looked at her. But on closer inspection, he had noticed her face was stress-free and her breathing rhythmic and peaceful. She had awakened with a start as he peered anxiously down at her.

'Oh Sam! Sorry. I haven't even started the tea.'

'Don't worry about that,' he'd assured her. 'I was scared you were feeling unwell again.'

She'd sighed. 'I'm fine, and you don't have to worry. We got through all that, and I won't be in that place again.'

She'd stood up slowly and given him a reassuring hug. For a minute, he'd felt a little light-headed; it was only then he realised he had been holding his breath. He knew how difficult she found the visits, but they both accepted it was a process they had to get through if they wanted to be parents.

When they were first married, he had often wished that Maria was a 'kick your shoes off, we will tidy up tomorrow' kind of person. But, with hindsight, he realises that having that kind of attitude might have prevented them being allowed to adopt their children. Sam sighs now with relief. Thankfully, they had been allowed, and that was all that mattered.

And Maria had always been a great mum to the girls. She had left school at 14 and gone straight to work in a china shop on the high street. When it closed for an hour in the middle of the day, Maria would walk home, have her lunch, then walk the two miles back to work, then do the same at closing time.

She had been strongly influenced by her own mother. Sam grinned as he remembered his mother-in-law becoming annoyed if he went outside to put the potato peelings in the bin, wearing a 'peeny'. 'Get him inside,' she would lament. 'The neighbours will see him!'

Maria had always longed to be a mother, and adoption had proved to be their only solution. But Sam would never forget the difficulties they had faced, and the dark years they had gone through.

He put his empty breakfast plate aside and sipped his cup of coffee, still lost in his thoughts. The adoption process had been so stressful for both of them, but they'd pulled together and grown close again. And how Maria had flourished as a mother!

She had always dressed the girls so well, making many of their clothes from scratch, using a much-treasured sewing machine which had belonged to her grandmother.

At times, she Had missed being able to go out to work and enjoy the company of adults, but women had not enjoyed so many childcare opportunities in those days. And Maria had been a traditional wife and mother.

Throughout the years, though, she had told him her day would come. And it did, when they opened the Cinnamon Café.

Chapter 13

Nadia

Ralf was the best brother anyone could wish for. I loved him. He always helped me, and I would have trusted him with my life.

He was older than me. When I think back on the photographs we had taken, we were dissimilar in features. He had a rounder face, and was always taller than me. When we smiled, though, our eyes shone – suggesting we lit up from the inside out. He always called me 'little one', which annoyed me as a little girl, but as we got older, I accepted it as I knew it was a playful term of affection.

Sundays were always my favourite days. We would go to church, come home, and my father would read. My mother would make sure all the arrangements for the following week were in order, to enable the household to run efficiently and effectively with minimum disruptions. We loved and respected our mother and father.

On the surface, our family was traditional and deeply religious. Ralf and I were encouraged from an early age to understand the importance of education, and were both very respectful of our culture. Our caste system was very important, and defined us in terms of our social standing. But we did not fully understand the caste system, and simply accepted our parents' word without question.

As part of the 'Rule Britannia' brigade, we had a good life. We were privileged, and both Ralf and I wanted for nothing. His aspirations were always to be a doctor, and eventually he went to train in London.

When we were growing up, we used to talk about the future and wonder what it would be like. I used to say to Ralf that I would miss him so much when it was time for him to go away to study, and we often borrowed books from the library to look at photographs of places in England. Places we never knew existed.

'What will I do without you here?' I would say, with tears in my eyes. I was so sad at the thought of him going away.

'Hush, little one, it's years away. Let's enjoy what we have,' he'd reply. Looking back, he was wise beyond his years. Or was it that we just had such a strong bond that he, like me, did not relish that time when we would be separated by such a distance.

I was fascinated by one particular book we looked at.

I asked Ralf, 'Where is Richmond-upon-the-Thames and Kew Gardens?'

'They are in London. And London is the capital city, just like Colombo.'

'Will it be the same size?'

'I don't know,' replied Ralf.

'Will the houses look the same?'

'Don't know.'

'Ralf, you don't know much,' I'd laugh, then he would chase me into the garden, both giggling. I loved my childhood. It was so simple, so clean, orderly, and safe.

We always knew that Ralf would go to London and become a doctor. Like me, he would enter an arranged marriage, and would be matched with a girl whose family would aid my father in his business world. My brother was happy with this as, like me, he had great respect for our mother and father's judgment. They had never failed either of us.

While I never fully understood the impact of this at that time, it was to have a life-changing impact on me in the future. High-caste families had more choices than others, due to their powerful influence within and outwith the community, and even the country we lived in.

'What is the caste system?' I asked Ralf one day.

'Look it up. Educate yourself, Nadia,' he told me.

So, I stomped out and pouted for a bit. Then I thought about what he said, and decided to ask if I could go to go to the school library and borrow some books. I was amazed at what I read. Caste had long existed in India, and many castes were traditionally associated with an occupation, such as high-ranking Brahmans; middle-ranking farmers and artisan groups, such as potters, barbers, and carpenters; and very low-ranking 'untouchable' leatherworkers, butchers, launderers, and latrine cleaners.

Members of higher-ranking castes tended, on the whole, to be more prosperous than members of lower-ranking castes. And many lower-caste people lived in conditions of great poverty and social disadvantage in our country.

While Ralf and I were aware from a very young age that we were to have an arranged marriage, I'd had no idea about all this other information. I knew we were certainly privileged, as all our schoolfriends' fathers were in politics, or were lawyers, teachers or doctors. But the information I read about what would make people 'untouchable' was what made me feel so sad.

It had a profound impact on me, so I went and talked to Ralf about this new-found knowledge, and was amazed at how much he was able to tell me.

'How do you know all this information?' I asked him. 'History lessons at school? What else do you know?'

He smiled. 'How would you like me to be your teacher, little one?'

'You could just tell me what I want to know and save me all this trouble.'

'Nadia, open your mind. You have so much to learn, but I cannot keep showing and telling you everything. You will enjoy learning once you start. You become thirsty for knowledge; it's amazing. I hope you realise that. I know up until now you have thought of school as just something you have to do. Change that concept in your mind, and the possibilities are endless.' The amusement in Ralf's eyes baited me to respond.

But I went away and thought about what he had said. And something inside me changed. I never again thought of school as just something I had to do.

Ralf was the kindest person I knew, and I looked up to him with great admiration. After all, he was my big brother, so I always thought of him as wiser.

Chapter 14

The power of education

Ralf's words – even to this day – made me view education differently.

Was that the turning point in my career choice? What was it about social justice that interested me? Why was there injustice for some, but not others? They were questions I would continue to ponder on for years to come.

My brother was my first real teacher. He taught me about life. He taught me about unconditional love. He was the best teacher I could ever hope for.

He was kind, and he was also passionate. He had worked out that beautiful dance between teacher and student. That beautiful transition and learning journey which students go on, where – if it's done well – there is a subtle switch of power, but both end up having ultimate respect for the other.

He thought it important that I learn about it myself, as he believed that was how education worked. 'I could tell you, and I can show you,' he explained, 'but if you research and do it for yourself, you will remember the important parts that interest you and can build on this throughout your life.'

Ralf then said, 'Teach him how to fish and you will feed him for a lifetime, as in the saying: *Feed a man for a day and he will not be hungry.*'

'What does that mean, Ralfy-Palfy? Go on, tell me, Mr Teacher, or is it Mr Smarty Pants? I don't even think I would like fishing.'

He laughed then. 'You don't literally have to go fishing, little one. It's a metaphor which means that you are helping people to survive using their own life skills.'

'I don't get it,' I replied.

'You will, one day.'

The next day, I went to the library and brought home more books., then went to my room and wrote down some notes. By comparing and thinking about what I was reading, I knew I was about to add to my knowledge.

I wrote:

'The chastity of women is strongly related to caste status. Generally, the higher ranking the caste, the more sexual control its women are expected to exhibit. Brahman brides should be virginal, faithful to one husband, and celibate in widowhood.

The matriarchs had an important social role within the family, they were responsible for ensuring their children were conditioned into the accepted standards of behaviours associated with such social standing, as well as ensuring that the next generation was produced within the boundaries of the class and caste system they were part of.

For the higher castes, such control of female sexuality helps ensure purity of lineage – of crucial importance to maintenance of high status.'

Chapter 15

Ralf

My thirst for knowledge could not be quenched. By the way our parents spoke to us, I already knew that there was an expectation for the higher castes to maintain control of female sexuality, as this helped ensure purity of lineage. This, along with the faith expectations, I now understood went hand-in-hand.

I did not even begin to wonder what would happen to you if you failed to maintain this. It was not something I would ever have to consider. I read book after book, and took notes, but it was difficult to understand everything.

I spoke to Ralf about this.

'Little one, you can't read reference books like that as though they were novels. You need to read a section and take notes.'

'Yes, I did that, Ralf. I read a bit and wrote notes on what that bit meant to me,' I said, looking very pleased with myself. 'I know now what you are talking about.'

Ralf pretended to bow and, with an equally big smile, said, 'My job is complete here, little one. I have taught you how to fish.'

'You mean, I am able to do this for myself now without your help?'

'Hoorah, hoorah,' he said, jokingly. 'You understand it now. I knew you would. You have potential, young lady.'

That, I believe, was a major turning point for me within the education system I was part of. I began to enjoy researching and loved reading about society. I really thrived within my culture. I worked hard at school, I listened, and began to imagine my brain was like a 'big library' where I would visualise taking out a book, adding some notes, then putting the book back on the shelf.

I liked it when I hadn't looked at a certain book for a while. I would pretend in my mind to blow the cobwebs off the neglected tome, then wag a finger and say to myself in a playful mocking voice, 'Tut, tut, tut, Nadia, have you been lazy?' Then I'd smile, because I knew I had not been lazy. 'Not in the least,' I would tell my subconscious. 'Look over here; I think my book on social policy is getting bigger and fatter by the week. What is that telling me?'

I believe it was guiding me towards something which interested me. I was thirsty for more information, and would talk about all my new-found knowledge at dinner time, when we chatted round the table.

To the outside world, my father was what they wanted him to be – he was the head of the house. He believed in respect, but he also actively encouraged his children to have a 'voice'. This made for interesting discussions, as we did not always agree, yet he believed that if we were allowed to discuss our thoughts respectfully, we would be able to build on that when we were adults in the working world, or take it forward into our own family values. The importance of listening to others, even if they have a conflicting opinion, was something I grew up valuing.

Ralfy-Palfy, how I miss you! Why did life have to become so difficult?

Chapter 16

Mafalda is gone forever

Mafalda, as I like to remember her, was taken from me just two weeks after she was born. I hope she was brought up knowing she was adopted, but what does that mean to a young child? And, if so, what was she told? That she grew in another woman's tummy? That she came to her new family because her adopted mother was not able to grow a baby in her tummy? That she was a darling adopted baby, and should be very proud of this?

If she was brought up with this knowledge and accepted it, did she share the information with others? Did she have any expectations? Would she ever want to find me? I wonder if she went through her school days with mixed emotions. It can't have been easy for her being a Ceylonese child in Britain in 1960. Poor little thing; it makes me so sad to think other children might have been mean to her. Why could I not have kept her, and made sure she didn't have to go through that?

Did she wear glasses? Were her clothes different? Did she go to a family with other children? What happened to her? I will never know. I WILL NEVER KNOW! The tears well up in my eyes as my tortured thoughts tumble over and over in my head. I blink the tears away and suppress the feelings of anger and frustration which are in danger of overwhelming me.

Mafalda was supposed to go to a Catholic family. I hope, if she did, that they loved her as much as I did – regardless of how she came to be. It was not her fault; she was, after all, an innocent by-product of my 'sin'.

How can she ever know how much I loved her and did not want to give her away? At that point in my life, I had no choices except the ones imposed on me by the people who were supposed to love and protect me.

I feel so sad carrying these thoughts and emotions with me on a daily basis. Such emotional baggage makes my heart feel so heavy in my body. The two halves I am now left with are not of me and Ralf, who made me so happy and complete. Instead, I am split into the professional woman seen by others, versus the broken woman I really am.

My life without Mafalda has never been complete. I constantly feel as if I have lost something, as though I am missing a limb. If only things had been different, would she have been with me now? What would she look like? Would she still look like me? Would we have a close bond? Would she hate me? Would she love me? I'll never know. I gave her life, but was not able to sustain that to support her through each stage of her growing up.

When she was taken away from me, I wrote a letter which I sent with her. The social worker in charge of my case promised me she would keep it as safe as she could. The woman was so kind to me. She did her best. I kept a copy of the letter for myself, as a reminder of how much of a disappointment I had become. All I had ever wanted was to do my best, to make my parents and my brother so very proud of me.

Why did I have to let her go? Why would no-one help me? I know the answers, yet this does not stop my heart from asking the questions.

I have held onto the letter for all these years, thinking naively that it would provide evidence if I was ever able to persuade my parents or Ralf to help me to keep my baby. But I've never told anyone about it or shown the letter to anyone. I have kept it safe, and only take it out to read every year on Mafalda's birthday.

Dear Miss K,

I received your letter in hospital. Sorry for the delay in replying. I was terribly upset about parting with the baby. I was compelled to give the child on the 28th to the adoption officer. She was taken to the home, which is very pathetic to think of. When I think of this, I keep crying, with nothing to be done. The nuns too did not like my keeping the child. They wanted me to do this and go back to my mother.

Since I am not allowed home, I wanted to keep her because I am responsible for bringing her into the world. I should never have had this baby. Poor thing, she has to go through any treatment given to her for my sins. I can never get over this. I keep praying. My mother wants me home, so I cannot work and have her. It is heart-breaking to think that she won't have anybody of her own in this country. What do you think of the home where coloured children are kept?

Thanks very much for the prayers you offered me. I had a diffi-cult time but never got over everything by the help of prayers. I had her on the 15th of this month and away in two weeks, which is heart-breaking. We are not used to giving away babies. This is the first time a thing like this happened in our family. My own sins have given me so much trouble

Yours sincerely,

Nadia

Even as I re-read the letter during my annual ritual in November, I feel the anger rise. I had complied at the time, still hoping for a different outcome. I was so very polite, begging and pleading with what I considered to be strong and persuasive language, in a desperate attempt to keep my baby. But, like many at that time, I was unable to rock the establishment. I never did, never will. The only true thing that was mine was so cruelly taken from me by people in authority, who thought they knew what was best for my baby. *MY* baby, not theirs!

I did not want to give her up. But I had to. I wanted my family to support me. Once she started moving inside me, I wanted to protect her – not punish her for the 'sin' I had committed.

In my heart, I knew I had not committed a sin. However, to my family, I had committed the worst possible crime. I had become pregnant by a man from a different caste, a different religion which was viewed very negatively by my caste. As a result, I could not be married to my intended, as I was no longer considered 'clean'. I felt like used goods – cast aside and forgotten about.

My crime, my only crime, was that I had thought I had a friend I could trust. He made me laugh, and I felt really good when I was around him. Stupidly, and naively, I lay with him.

Chapter 17

Shattered dreams

As a young girl, I was chauffeur-driven everywhere as it was not considered safe for me to go anywhere unaccompanied. I didn't object, though, as I knew my father's prominent job meant I had to be respectful of the choices he made for me.

Women within my culture were not always viewed positively, but I was lucky. My family adored me. As is common in eastern cultures, I was to have an arranged marriage. This is where the two families come together, and the children do have a choice – to a degree – about their potential suitor. The young man I was to be married to was the son of one of my father's business partners. This is very common; the joining together of the two families is often to support business matters as well as family tradition.

When I first saw him, our eyes met and I felt an emotional exchange between us. This made me happy, as he made me feel comfortable even before we had even introduced ourselves. He was very tall, thin in build, and had oval brown eyes like my mother, yet when he spoke he sounded like my father.

He was kind in the words he used to interact with me. He complimented me on my clothes, saying the turquoise blue reminded him of the ocean and its calming effects. He said my hair smelled like flowers, and told me I was like a ray of sunshine – bright, vibrant, warm, and comforting. I was completely and utterly convinced I had met my match. Together, we would go on to have a family after we married. We would live a traditional life. Even though I had been educated in Colombo, I would give up work, but would be content to do this as we appeared to be completely compatible. There was an instant attraction, which I hoped would last a lifetime. My life seemed idyllic.

Mansui, our chauffeur, was a young man who was not of the same faith as my family. He had been given the job because my father was impressed by his determination to succeed.

Although he was always very polite to me, sometimes while he was driving our eyes would occasionally meet, but I never gave it a thought. He was happy to ask me all about my studies and always seemed interested, so every journey we would chat and soon a friendship began to develop. When I answered his questions about my studies, he would reply that I was a fountain of knowledge. I liked this description, and it made me laugh. He said when I laughed that my whole face lit up like the sunshine.

My father trusted him. I trusted him. He came with good references from his previous employer – an influential local family – and I had no reason to doubt him. He was cheerful, fun, and reliable, and I always looked forward to our journeys.

One February afternoon, as I was being driven home, he took a detour. When I asked why, he said he wanted to show me something very beautiful. He had been thinking about showing me this for some time, he said, and was unsure if I would like it.

I was intrigued. 'What is it?'

'A surprise.'

'Tell me. Tell me.'

'No, wait and see.' He paused. 'Do you want to see?'

'Yes,' I replied eagerly.

He took the car up a long road then stopped. There, in front of us, was the most spectacular view. It was breathtakingly beautiful.

He got out of the car and got into the back seat beside me. As we sat close together, he leaned across and pointed out of the window at several landmarks.

'Mansui,' I said, 'this is amazing. Thank you. I will remember this for the rest of my life.'

He smiled. 'I thought you would love it.'

Suddenly, I was very aware of his presence. Before I could react, he turned towards me and kissed me. I was totally taken aback, as I knew I had only ever been friendly and polite towards him.

His kiss became more urgent. He had always been so kind, and I liked and trusted him. So, I did not resist his kiss, and we lay down together on the back seat of the car. But it was beginning to feel uncomfortable, so I asked him to stop and he did. He then looked at me again and began to kiss me with an urgency. I was taken aback at this, but found that I was overcome by an emotion I had never experienced before. In the heat of the moment, he and I were lying semi-naked in the back of the car. He told me he loved me, but I asked him to stop. I knew that heavy petting would still result in pregnancy, and I was afraid that we had gone too far.

I liked Mansui but not in the same way that he liked me. I explained that we must never do this again, as I was to be married, and it was very important that I did not disrespect my family's wishes.

He was annoyed, saying he loved me and would look after me, so I tried to reason with him.

'Mansui, I am in love with someone else. I have never been with a man, but I will only ever be with my husband. Our kissing and cuddling today has been a big mistake. Why can't you understand, you are just my friend, and things have gone too far today?'

'Just your friend?'

'Yes.'

He was still angry. 'When we kissed and cuddled, did you not feel love?'

'No,' I replied, as kindly as possible. 'I have found love in the man I am to marry. Now, please take me home.'

He got back into the driver's seat and drove for what seemed like a very long time. He was very quiet, and I began to feel more and more uneasy.

'Please take me home,' I repeated.

'We are nearly there.'

'Where?' I asked, looking frantically out of the window.

'HOME!' he shouted. 'Where you want to go'

Eventually, he stopped the car near our house and said quietly, 'I want to talk to you.'

'I'm so sorry, Mansui, this was a big mistake. We are friends, nothing else. What happened was a big mistake on my part. I do not wish to hurt you, as you are my friend.'

He started to get into the back of the car with me again. 'I want to talk to you, Nadia.,

I knew I had to get out of there. My inner self was warning me that I could be danger, as he was still angry. Normally, the car doors were locked for security once you were inside, but he had unlocked the door when he started to climb into the back.

I quickly opened my door and began to run. I did not know where I was, and I was frightened. But the 'fight or flight' reflexes helped me to run much faster than normal and I looked wildly around me for an escape route.

Eventually, I came to a path which led me towards our home and I raced back there, my heart thudding, almost out of breath. I was frightened, but I did not know why. I had been so foolish to think that Mansui knew we were friends. I had been stupid to kiss and cuddle him and lay in the back of the car with him.

I started to pray, desperately hoping that I had not sinned. I hoped God would understand that I had made a terrible mistake.

Inside the house, I went straight to my room, closed the door, and cried. What had I done? We just kissed and cuddled and lay in the back of the car? What had I done? Did I lead him on? Oh God, please help me, I think I may have sinned? I knew, as part of a high caste Catholic family, that sex before marriage was a 'sin'. Oh my God, help me. Who would believe me? Ralf.

I ran a bath, and stayed there, feigning illness to avoid dinner. Then I went to bed. When I got up in the morning, I asked Ralf to ride in the car with me. I must never be alone with Mansui again; it would be wrong.

Ralf laughed and rubbed my head, joking, 'What is it now, little one?'

I knew I had to be brave. I had to get him to help me. So, I told him what had happened.

He looked at me in dismay, then said he would deal with it but he needed time to think. He came with me in the car, but after we had driven for about five minutes, Ralf told the chauffeur to stop the car for a minute then he got out.

He dragged Mansui from the car, and then began punching him. I have never seen my brother so angry.

I heard him say to Mansui, 'What do you think you are playing at?'

'Nothing,' he replied. 'I love her and want to marry her.'

'You know that's not possible, I hope you did not cross a line between friendship and anything else.'

'Yes. I did,' Mansui said proudly. 'I know she will love me, you wait and see.'

Then he took a swipe at Ralf, but my brother was much faster, and he knocked Mansui to the ground. I was so scared. I was way out my depth. I knew I had been very stupid to let him kiss and cuddle me, and to lie with him in the car.

Ralf was true to his word; he *did* come up with a solution. He told my father I had been over-friendly with the chauffeur. My mother was annoyed. She agreed to Mansui being given my £6000 inheritance as well as a new car, if he agreed to just disappear. I never saw him again.

But he left me a package behind. A package which would arrive in this world nine months later, unaware of the circumstances surrounding its existence.

For me, life was never the same. I began to feel sick. I began to look different. I bathed daily, and scrubbed and scrubbed to rid myself of the dirty way I felt. I was so ashamed, but there was no-one I could tell.

Even Ralf looked at me differently, as if I had encouraged Mansui. But I hadn't. Yet I had no credibility, and no-one understood. I could tell no-one that I had made a mistake with Mansui. I cried. I cried. I cried.

Ralf had always enjoyed an unspoken closeness with my mother, and he trusted her judgement on everything. They discussed the situation, and arrangements were made to redeem the family's good honour and remove any traces related to my sin.

My marriage arrangements were cancelled. I was so sad. I hurt so deep inside. It felt as though a part of me died that day in February. Everyone looked at me with disdain, and I felt ashamed, hurt, and sad. In some way, I also felt sorry for Mansui, as he had said he loved me. But I knew I never loved him; I really did think all we had was friendship.

Ralf had been back at home that February because he had finished his studies and had secured employment. Our family was so proud of him. February fell between the two rainy seasons at home, and the warm temperature provided an ideal contrast to the British weather he had left behind. My beautiful sister in-law had also come with him for a holiday. I had been so excited, as I was going to get the chance to get to know her better.

I hoped we would be close, not just because we were sisters-in-law, but because she was Ralf's wife. I had always loved him so much, and hoped we could spend many more summers together for the rest of our lives. In the first week of their stay, I had been able to connect well with her. Like him, she oozed happiness and contentment. I was happy, too – until my terrible sin.

Once my mistake happened, it was decided that Ralf and his wife would return to the UK as planned, and I would follow to visit them for a much-needed vacation on completion of my studies. That was the story everyone would be told, to ensure complete discretion and avoid any shame touching my family.

Chapter 18

Where did you go, Ralf?

I felt more betrayed by Ralf than by anyone else in the whole messy situation.

Sure, he dealt with Mansui, but the way my brother looked at me from that day on sent shivers down my spine. He of all people should have known that it had been a terrible mistake, and that I was deeply sorry for betraying and dishonouring our family. We had always been like two halves of the one. We'd enjoyed a special bond, and he had always been the best brother I could have asked for. But now, he was not happy with me, and it meant I no longer had anyone I could confide in.

I felt as though I no longer had any family; I had already lost their emotional support. I had no-one. What was I to do?

Ralf did what was expected of him as the male member of the family at that time. I was shipped off to stay with him and his wife in the UK, and he was given the task of 'dealing' with the situation. But our relationship was stilted, and he dealt with me in the way he might with one of his patients – decisive, matter-of-fact, and emotionally detached.

My journey to the UK was very traumatic, and I arrived at their home in Richmond-upon-Thames exhausted and tired, hoping and praying that he and his beautiful wife would be kind to me. Even though their marriage had been arranged,

I could tell that there was a certain contentment and warmth between them, and they appeared happy together.

But my hopes and prayers were not answered. As soon as I was shown to my room, I felt a sudden coldness despite the house being warm. I looked at my sister in-law and saw no emotion or compassion in her eyes; instead, a stern, controlled look met mine.

'Welcome to our home,' she said, making me feel like an inconvenience to their settled life.

'Thank you,' I said respectfully, trying to hold back the tears which stung my eyes.

'I do hope you will have a pleasant stay.' There was no warmth or emotion behind the words.

'Yes. Thank you very much for having me as a guest in your home.'

With another cool response, she said, 'Dinner will be served at 7.30. That will give you time to settle in and freshen up.'

'Yes, of course.' My words were barely a whisper. 'Thank you again.'

As I looked round the room, the loneliness hit me like a sad cape which seemed to fall on me from a great height. I tried to fight the feeling, and I did as instructed. I freshened up, then went down to dinner. It was a silent affair. There was no conversation apart from reiterating the welcome.

'Welcome to our home, Nadia. I hope you have a pleasant stay,' said Ralf.

'Oh Ralf. I am so happy to see you,' I said tearfully.

'As I said, Nadia, welcome to our home. I hope you have a pleasant stay,' was his cool reply.

I lowered my head and quietly muttered, 'Thank you.'

If the situation had been different, I would have loved to be staying here with my brother and getting to know my sister-in-law properly.

She had excellent taste, and the house was beautifully decorated. The bedroom they had given me was delightful, with gentle colours on the walls and expensive soft furnishings of bold colours, which reminded me of home. The dazzling quilted bedroom set had the luxurious look and feel of silk, boldly displaying rich jewel tones. The combined quilted squares of shimmering coloured material in cerise, pale blue, green, terracotta, purple, and red, stood boldly to attention on the bed.

It appeared seamless and made to perfection, and I knew it must be expensive when I touched the fabric.

On the wall hung an expensive picture which perfectly depicted our country of origin, particularly the ornate detail of the elephant. It was stunning. The picture was classic bronze and terracotta, and glittered like gold; the ornate jewels matched the bed set. There were small diamond-shaped mirrors embossed and so delicately woven into the ornate cover which was strategically placed over the elephant. There was a glimmer in the detail which represented the band round the cover.

On closer inspection there were green, red, terracotta, and yellow jewels which complemented the gold finger-shaped detail and gold balls. Ironically, the elephant appeared to be happily trumpeting.

I would lie in bed at night and look at the picture, trying to imagine I was back in Ceylon with my loving family around me, enjoying a family meal the way we used to.

Ralf was clearly a successful and respected paediatrician, but every time I was summoned to his front room, which he used like an office, our conversations were business-like and lacking in any emotion.

And when I looked at my sister-in-law with sad eyes, desperate for some kind of connection, her only response was, 'Nadia, please do as you are asked.'

I was summoned to Ralf's 'office' every time any kind of decisions had been made. On one occasion, he told me that arrangements had been made for me to go away to have my baby; that way, my indiscretion would disappear.

I was heartbroken. 'I know this was my fault, Ralf, and I am so sorry, but is there no other way?' I pleaded.

'Be quiet and listen,' he snapped. 'This is what will happen. You will take the night train; you will have your baby; you will leave it; you will then come back, when I am satisfied that no mistakes have been made.'

'What do you mean *mistakes*?' I asked.

'Any traces of the bastard.' His very words were hard and cold, and another shiver went down my spine. When had he become so mean?

'I will then arrange your passage back to be with Mother and Father. It should be a clean and simple affair. The Home has been given a donation to ensure your discretion remains a secret, and you must never tell anyone of this, do you understand? People at home believe you have come to London to visit us.'

I nodded. My baby was to be adopted. Apparently, I had no choice in the matter. But I could not help the tears coursing down my face as I sobbed.

'Stop that, this minute,' he ordered, making no effort to comfort me. 'I will not have this.' His eyes were hard and cold, like the steel bars on my bedroom window.

On another occasion, when I was being escorted to the front room, my sister-in-law told me, 'You should never have done what you did. Now we all have to pay for your actions.'

I was so angry, I could not look at her. *Did she really think I enjoyed being so naïve and making such a stupid mistake?* But I was a visitor in her home, so I must obey and not be dishonourable.

So, I did the only thing I thought would work. I stayed in my room and refused to communicate or go along with any of his plans. I would not obey him. I would not let my baby be taken away. It was not my child's fault that I had 'sinned'.

I tried so very hard. I did not eat with them. I locked the door. I stayed in my room. When I thought the house was empty, I would creep out, wash, then sneak downstairs to the kitchen, where a kindly servant would make me a sandwich then slide it over as she left the room. She made sure to make no eye contact, and no conversation. While this was a kindly act, I was very aware that it must never be perceived as if she were helping me. If they found out, she would lose her job for aiding and abetting the prisoner upstairs. *So, why was she risking everything? Had she been through a similar situation?* I would never know, and she would never tell me.

I naively thought I was outsmarting them all. How foolish and immature I was.

Angrily, my brother summoned me again one morning and told me I was to go on the next train to the Home.

'No,' I told him.

'Then you leave me no choice. You will stay in a hostel, where you will require to survive on national assistance of £3-10s-0d.'

I watched in silence as he began writing to someone to let them know of my decision. It was as though he was writing a prescription for a patient.

His letter to the adoption society was stern, and totally lacking in empathy.

Dear Madam

I regret very much to inform you that my sister has let me down very badly at this last moment, and now refuses the place in the Home which you have arranged for her. She is in a disturbed state of mind, and has probably made this hasty decision not realising the gloomy consequences.

I am sorry for all this inconvenience to you.

Under the present circumstance, I have no alternative but to postpone her trip. This last-minute decision has completely upset the plans.

I regret very much that she will not be able to keep the appointment with you on the 21st at 11am.

If, however, she changes her mind, I shall send her on the night train on the 23rd.

I am very upset at this present state of affairs, and shall thank you to keep this place reserved for her till you hear from me. I quite realise your position at the moment. Please excuse me for attempting to abuse your generosity.

Hopefully, she will meet with you on the 24th or 25th.

Yours faithfully,

R Selon

Clearly, Ralf thought that it would break my spirit to go from luxury to poverty. *Did he really think he could do this to me?* Yes, he did. It was so hard for me not to say, 'Ok, you win.'

I left the house that night and went to the hostel. But I was so scared. What would I do on my own, in this strange city, with a baby? It was 1960, after all. Every night, I pleaded with God to help me. But my prayers were never answered.

I felt completely and utterly destroyed. I felt so weak and vulnerable.

I never wanted to see or speak to Ralf again. I hated them all, and would never go home. I would never forgive them, never ever, for as long as I lived.

Chapter 19

From everything to nothing

I thought naïvely that the hostel would be a bit worse than Ralf and his wife's house. And it was. I was so very scared.

The person at the front desk spoke kindly to me when I went to register, and told me to go to Room 24, where I would find a four-bedded room. As I made my way along the corridor, it felt cold; the smell of dampness was disguised by the smell of washing powder as I passed the laundry room. The industrial washing machine sounded noisy.

A man passed me in the corridor and smiled. I smiled back. Then a woman and a baby passed. I smiled. She smiled, and I began to feel less frightened. But this was not a home. It felt strange. I felt vulnerable, as I was not used to fending for myself, but it was me and my baby now, and I was determined I would make this work. Almost as determined as I had been to remove my psychological barrier to education when we were younger.

Just remember, Nadia, this is for you and your baby, I kept telling myself. My room appeared comfortable enough at first. I was told my bunk was the top one, which was difficult for someone as small as me to get up to, but I made up my mind I would manage. I would succeed. This was my chance to put my faith in God. I knew He would protect me if I said my prayers. That night, I prayed to survive this ordeal. I prayed that I could keep my baby. I prayed that God would show me the light in this dark situation.

Night and day, I stayed in the hostel except when I had to go and sign on to receive my national assistance. It wasn't much money, but I did not spend a lot so should be able to manage.

For the first few days, people were allowed to stay inside the hostel to settle in. But when I went to pay my rent money, I was told that as of the next day I had to be out all day and only come back in the evenings. *Where could I go?*

I went to the library. Then I wandered around shops, looking at clothes for my baby. Blue, pink, and lemon clothes; there was not a great deal of variety. One day, I went into one of the famous department stores in London, wandering slowly from department to department.

My eyes were immediately drawn to a display of baby blankets. It was like a magnet; I was drawn to them. Without thinking, I touched the Portuguese easy-care, satin-bound cover. It felt so soft and comforting that I suddenly felt homesick. I felt the emotion rise in me but managed to regain my composure before a friendly shop assistant came over.

'Hello,' she said brightly, 'can I be of assistance?'

'I'm just looking,' I mumbled.

'Oh, these are new in. They feel so authentic, don't you think?'

I nodded. 'Yes, they do indeed.'

'What colour would you like?'

Before I could answer, she went on, "We have lemon or cream, which is neutral for either a boy or a girl. We also have rose pink, or pale blue.'

'Thank you,' I tried again, 'I am just looking.'

She wasn't to be fobbed off. 'Is it a gift?' she asked. 'Is it for a boy or a girl?'

My answer was an honest one. 'I don't know.'

I began to feel uneasy and moved slowly away, thanking her for her assistance. I thought I heard her tut as I left, and mutter 'time-waster' to another assistant.

Back outside, I walked and walked. Then I came across a little coffee shop, The Cinnamon Café. I went into the café at least twice that day, to drink a cup of tea and to feel the warmth.

It was difficult. It was lonely. But I would do this for my baby. I felt sure God would guide me to a solution. Surely He loved the little children, as it said in the psalms. So, He would help me to find the best thing for me and my baby.

I waited. I prayed. I waited. I prayed.

Nothing.

I waited. I prayed. I waited. I prayed.

Nothing happened.

I started to feel more alone; even lonelier than I'd felt in Ralf's house.

The hostel was basic. In the early evening, there were young families coming and going, but the atmosphere changed as the evening wore on.

Men and women would go out – to work? To meet friends? I had no idea. Then there would be the sound of children crying. Were they ill? Unhappy? Or did children just cry at times, even though they had been fed and changed and were loved?

As night fell, drunken men and women could be heard talking loudly and aggressively, then someone would shout, 'Be quiet or we will get put out.' There would be a thud as someone banged against the door a few times, then voices.

'What number is that? Can't see it, look again.'

'Oh, it's 24. Is that the one?'

'No, it's 42 we want.'

The hostel was never quiet, and I found myself cat-napping rather than getting a proper sleep.

As the days dragged on, I felt another change in my spirit. I began to feel so desperately alone and wondered what would become of me. I went from hope to despair. It was horrible. I started to question myself: had this happened, or had that happened? Had I dreamt that? Did I hear that? I was becoming disorientated.

God, please don't reject me when I need you most, I prayed. *I am a woman in desperate need of help, alone in a city I hardly know.*

My thoughts and dreams became distorted, and I experienced terrible nightmares which would wake me up, feeling frightened and alone. The person in the bunk below told me to shut up or they would shut me up.

Was there any way out of this? What choices did I have?

My thoughts grew darker, and I wondered whether my baby and I would be better off dead. I felt that might be the easiest option, and I started to plan the end of my life. Maybe then Ralf and his wife would be sorry for their actions. Maybe my parents would regret their treatment of me. As I grew more and more depressed and sad, my plan seemed like my only option.

And I was going to do it. I really was. But I did not have the courage to follow my plan through. God would be even angrier with me for committing not just one sin, but also for the mortal sin I was contemplating.

I felt completely overwhelmed; dead or alive, there was nothing to be done for the sin I had committed. I was alone, and I could not possibly survive in the hostel. It was then that I finally submitted.

I found myself walking up a road. As I dragged my weary body along, I realised that I was walking towards Ralf's street and back to his house.

Before long, it had all been organised. I was put on a train... and the rest is history. I hate it when people say that. Because the history I am part of is a sad time for mothers and babies. I know this. I have felt it with every bone of my body; the feelings of hopelessness; the happiness associated with hope that if you have faith it may all work out.

But nothing was working out as I had hoped and prayed it would. Neither Ralf nor his wife appeared to care. I had no real choices, yet I still clung to the belief that I would not give up my baby. I would do everything in my power to prevent this terrible miscarriage of justice.

Chapter 20

Kavindi – Ralf's wife

My Ralf, I know him so well. How did Nadia not understand that he was not a 'typical' man, whatever that means? I loved her through him – all his memories of their childhood; the fun they had; the bond they shared. It was strange. I thought I would resent her for this, but I was wrong. I admired them both so much, for they were truly two of a kind, and enjoyed a special brother-sister relationship.

Ralf loved his 'little one', and she adored her 'Ralfy Palfy'. Hearing that out of context could sound stupid. But his mother told me that when Ralf and Nadia were young, if you ever met them, you would never know the bond they shared. They were upstanding in the community and behaved in an impeccable manner wherever they went.

He was a man of great integrity, and defied the cultural expectations at that time of how a man should behave. Spending time with his family that summer, I quickly realised how much Ralf admired his parents and would always respect and honour their wishes.

Nadia told me that he had been a great scholar, always hungry for knowledge. As a young man, he began to adapt to fit in with the expectations within the wider community, but very few knew the real Ralf the way his family and Nadia did.

I remember he told me once that some of his friends at the cricket club would try to typify him, and make suggestions that he was like this or that. It had amused him that they clearly did not know him as well as they thought. The one he thought most amusing was when someone had described him as 'a man's man'.

He was the complete opposite. He was a very kind, caring brother towards his 'little one', and told her often that he would always be there for her, come hell or high water. So, it did not surprise me that he was particularly demonstrative towards me – behind closed doors, of course. From our first meeting, we had a very special emotional connection. A love to defy all others; we were destined to be together. Soul mates, with a great sense of spirituality rooted in our faith.

Ralf oozed a kindness and compassion when we were alone. As a couple, we would never display our emotions publicly, but that was something I respected in him. We were complete.

So I was genuinely not prepared for what would happen to us. We had gone back to Ceylon for a much welcome rest once Ralf had finished his studies. That was to be 'our summer to remember'. And it certainly was – but not for the reasons I'd expected. The fallout from that time would, unbeknown to me, last a lifetime.

At first, the visit was so relaxing. It felt good to feel the heat of the sun on my back. A heat so different from the country I now called home. I enjoyed spending time with my sister-in-law, and could understand why she and Ralf were so close. They were like two halves of one, complementing each other perfectly. Their relationship was everything Ralf had described and more. We all felt truly blessed.

I felt confident that, with Ralf's support, I would settle and eventually call Britain home. I felt safe and loved, and

I knew Ralf would look after us, as he had always done. He was the main breadwinner, and looked after our finances; I was a homemaker, a doctor's wife held in high esteem by the community where Ralf had taken up post.

We were happy and strong, and ready to settle into a secure financial and emotionally stable life.

Early one morning, not long before we left Ceylon, I thought I heard a soft knock on the door.

Then Ralf whispered to me, 'Kavindi, I am going with Nadia to school this morning.'

I must have fallen asleep again, and when I did wake up, Ralf was in bed beside me. I must have been dreaming that he had accompanied Nadia to school. *Why would he do that?*

Chapter 21

Kavindi's pain

Ralf told me later that he did everything he could to help Nadia, who had committed the ultimate sin. He had tried to reason with their parents, pleading with them to support her, and pointing out that the prime minister's mother-in-law was a single parent. But they would not listen to him.

They spoke of the dishonour; of going against her caste; of the church's view of unwed mothers; and that sex before marriage was a crime.

And they told Ralf to deal with it. Nadia was to be sent to Britain to stay with us, and they expected him to organise everything, to make sure she complied with the arrangements at any cost, then to send her back home – alone – to them in Ceylon. After that, her indiscretion would never be spoken about again within the family.

He really did try to reason with them on her behalf, arguing that Nadia had been very naive and foolish but was a good person. He pleaded on her behalf and begged for their support. *'Please don't do this to her. Surely you, of all people, should know she would never deliberately dishonour the family. She has made one terrible big mistake. We will take the baby as part of my family.'*

They would not listen to any of his pleas. They were firm; they stood strong. They were his parents. And he obeyed.

But my husband was heartbroken at what he was being asked to do to his 'little one'. On one occasion, I overheard him in the front room crying and pleading with his parents, to no avail. He was to act like the head of the family, to remove all emotion, and deal with this situation.

As an honourable man, Ralf would not disobey his parents, in spite of the agony which he felt. On a few occasions, I have come down in the morning to find him asleep in his office, clutching a treasured photograph of himself and Nadia laughing. They looked so young, so close, so happy... so lucky.

But any time I challenged Ralf, he would not speak of his feelings. I tried so many different ways to get him to talk about his pain, but he got angry and told me never to mention it again. So, I never did.

I loved Ralf from the moment we met. He was handsome, had the same shape of eyes as his mother, and was similar – yet different – from his little sister. The main difference was the shape of his face; his was rounder. But, like her, his eyes shone when he was happy. He reminded me of the sunshine – warm, relaxing, safe. I remember after I met him, I would lie in bed and think how much I really liked his smiling face.

Each time we met, he would look at me and tell me something funny. We would touch each other affectionately – behind closed doors, of course – and laugh and laugh till our sides hurt. He told me I was everything he had hoped for, that we would never go to sleep on an argument, and that he had faith we would live a full and happy life together.

He told me that we were blessed to have family, to have our faith, to be part of a good caste system. I remember him saying, 'What more could a man ask for?'

And I believed him, I really did. *Was I just young and stupid?*

I tried. I really tried to help him deal with his pain and sorrow, but he kept shutting me out. It was a gradual moving away from each other. *How does this happen when you love someone so much you think you will die if you are no longer together as one?*

How long did it take for him to no longer laugh? I have no idea, though I have thought and thought about this over the years. Even down to the ridiculous level of trying to put a date and a time on it. All I know is it that it was during and after the Nadia situation that he stopped laughing the way he used to. Like that carefree man whom I loved and adored more than words can say.

He could disguise it. Of course, he laughed. But the laughter just never reached his eyes any more. He went from being the sunshine in a bright blue sky, to a man who was occasionally illuminated like the moon within a dark sky. He looked sad and deep in thought, particularly at times when he was not working.

When our babies were born, Ralf showed little interest. He worked longer and longer hours. In truth, we all lost something because of Nadia.

How I hate her. I hate her for the life I've lost. She broke his heart and he never recovered. 'What about me?' I would say at night when we were in bed. But he would not answer. He would simply turn off his bedside lamp and go to sleep.

I wanted to leave him so many times. I really did. Yet, I could not. I would never dishonour my family the way Nadia did.

The way she behaved when she came to stay with us was awful. She was stubborn. She would not obey Ralf. She behaved like a spoiled brat. *But why?* After all, it was she who had committed the worst possible crime – by becoming pregnant.

Why was her baby so important? She was even prepared to go and live on her own in a hostel. She tried that stupid isolation act – like that was going to work. *Why did she not just obey Ralf? Did she really think he'd willingly send her away? If she did, she must be more stupid than I thought?*

I used to envy their close relationship. Not any more. Her actions destroyed my life with my husband, and we never recovered. Adoption destroyed our family – immediate and extended. We never recovered from the atrocity which happened so very far away in another country.

Before he retired, and after the children left home, we tried to move our lives forward and make the best of a bad job. But my heart had been broken in 1960 – that was the year I lost my husband. He was no longer the man he was destined to become. He changed beyond belief.

When he put Nadia on that train to have her baby adopted, he cried like his heart was breaking. But he never saw Nadia again.

Just before he died, he asked me if I thought she had ever forgiven him.

I replied sadly, 'I don't know, Ralf, but I do know our children never had the father you could have been.'

Chapter 22

What happened to you, Mansui?

Leaving behind his job as a chauffeur was the saddest day of his life.

Mansui had a drive to be successful from a young age, no matter what and how long it would take. When he arrived to work for Nadia's family, he knew he had arrived and that this was the job which was to fulfil him. Delighted to be working for such a gentle and caring family, he enjoyed observing the close relationship between Nadia and her brother.

Brought up in a loving, respectful environment, Mansui was an extremely private person. His family was very proud that he was working for successful people, and he valued and respected his position. So, what possessed him to overstep the line that day? It was a question he continued to ask himself for many years.

He was so angry with himself that on that one occasion he had allowed his emotions to rule his head. The disloyalty he felt towards the family was overwhelming at times. No matter how hard he tried, he could not shift the sadness that came over him. It took him many years to put that terrible atrocity and his lack of professional judgement behind him.

For a long time, it would eat away at his inner peace, and he suffered terrible nightmares. In one, he was caught in the car with a big hand holding him down. It was like he was being literally pushed through the roof of the car. Harder and harder he was being pushed, until he felt like he was suffocating. Then he felt the sensation of the cold metal against his skin, and he woke up screaming, 'I am sorry! So very sorry!'

He could still remember Nadia's elated face at seeing the beautiful view. She looked so gracious, happy, and content. He had loved the friendship and laughter they shared. *So, what possessed him to cross the line?*

And afterwards… Nadia looked so sad and broken. She'd had no idea that his feelings had changed towards her. Why had he thought she knew? She had never given him any indication to suggest this.

It had been a completely overwhelming surge of emotion that made Mansui kiss and caress her, and ask her to lie in the back of the car with him. He should have stopped, but by then it was too late. He was not to know at that moment in time that his illusion of a perfect life would be forever shattered. The ideal life he had carved out for himself disappeared out the door the moment Nadia ran away from him, like he was some deranged animal who was going to attack and harm her. He would never forget that as long as he lived.

Mansui had never had any desire to hurt Nadia; she was such a special person. There was always such lightness in her tone of voice, suggesting her complete trust and faith in him as a human being. If only he hadn't taken her to see that view.

'Mansui, this is both amazing and stunning,' she had said. 'I will remember this for the rest of my life.'

He, too, has remembered those moments for his whole life – but for all the wrong reasons.

In the early days, he tried to write so many letters of apology, but the words seemed trite and he never sent them. He had felt embarrassed after the fight with Ralf, and insulted that the family thought giving him £6000 and a new car was acceptable.

He had loved Nadia, without question. He would have accepted his responsibilities and married her. He was sure she might have grown to love him. But although he was good enough to be the family chauffeur, he would never have been considered acceptable as a son-in-law. For a start, their contrasting faith beliefs would have been a huge barrier. Added to that, he had crossed the line, where chastity was of utmost importance to her family.

He could only hope that she had recovered from the ordeal and gone on to enjoy a full life.

Initially, his guilt prevented him from using the money the family had given him, and he decided to sell the car. But he pretended for a long time that he was still working for Nadia's family, as he knew he would arouse his mother's suspicion if he suddenly returned to live with her.

On one visit home after very many months of pretence, his mother asked him directly, 'Mansui, something is not right. What is it?"

'What do you mean?' he shrugged.

He said nothing else, but looked into her sad eyes and simply nodded.

She told him, 'If you can't fix whatever it is honestly, without dishonouring our family name, then you must try to put it behind you and move on with your life. You appear to be a broken man, for whatever reason. Love, I assume. Please deal with it, Mansui, as your regrets are eating away at you from within.'

They never spoke of it again, but that proved to be the turning point in his life.

It took him some time to be able to move on from his guilt and regrets. But with his mother's support – and the money from Nadia's family – he was able to eventually open a café in Colombo. It proved to be a successful venture and, as his business grew, he eventually opened several more cafes in other areas.

He has always been grateful for his mother's help and strength of character. He so easily could have stayed a broken man had she not known him so well and offered those words of wisdom. His mother never judged him. She loved him, and forgave him for something she knew nothing about.

Mansui is now no longer the raven-haired young man who challenged Ralf that day so many years ago. Now a distinguished gentleman with white hair to complement his ageing cinnamon skin, there is a deep sadness in his eyes. And the wealthy businessman would trade all his success for the love of a very special friend who he betrayed so long ago.

Chapter 23

Nadia and Mafalda

Iknew in my heart that when I left the mother and baby home, I would never see my baby again.

I was given only a few minutes with my beautiful daughter to say goodbye.

'Goodbye, my baby. I will never forget you. Do you hear me, Mafalda?' I whispered.

She was fast asleep. I gazed at her sweet face and tried so very hard to take in every detail of her delicate features, her whole being, from her face to her feet. I was frantically trying to transport the information to my head, but it was not happening. The link between my heart and head was blocked.

The hot tears which had initially blurred my vision began flowing down my cheeks at such a pace that I felt sure if I looked in the mirror, two craters would be visible on my skin. My brain could not compute the information I so desperately wanted to save; my heart had a pain so intense that it felt like it was about to explode out of my body.

The soft blanket which Mafalda was lying on was becoming damp with my tears, so I moved it over gently and carefully, trying not to disturb her. I'd had to become disciplined to help hide my daily pain, or the nuns would have stopped me having any contact with my baby.

Little Mafalda gently opened her eyes.

My heart lurched. 'Hello, my baby. I am your mother. Please look at me and remember me always.' I whispered to her, my eyes never leaving her little face. 'Never forget I am your mother. I loved you so much that I have given birth to you. Unfortunately, even though it breaks my heart, I am not being allowed to keep you.'

Mafalda looked at me in the same way as she had done on the previous thirteen days since her birth. I could only hope my face would be imprinted on her brain as her first carer, one who loved her so very, very much.

Normally, when there was no-one else around, I would lift her and hold her close, to continue to establish the bond which was developing between the two of us. But at that moment, I decided it would be unfair for my little Mafalda to sense my acute emotional pain on what would be our last day together. We had been one entity for the past nine months, and this forced separation was just so unbearably cruel for us both.

I gently opened her little hand and curled it around my finger; the connection was so strong. My baby held on. *Was she telling me not to leave her? Would she be alone and afraid after today?* After a full minute, I carefully and slowly removed my finger. Mafalda briefly held her hand motionless, then made a small, jerky movement, before she relaxed and put her hand gently back under her ear and closed her eyes. She went back to sleep.

I will never ever see her again, I kept telling myself. My brain couldn't take it in, and a heart-wrenching sob escaped from my body, in spite of my desperate efforts to stifle it. I felt my throat constrict, and the tears began flowing again, while my mind whirled as I tried to take in the full impact of what was about to happen. I was rooted to the spot, hoping for some kind of miracle that the situation could be reversed; that my family would call and say Mafalda and I could come home together; that my parents had forgiven me and could understand the importance of this young life.

The room was bare, cold, and unwelcoming. It had a wooden floor and a line of cots, and nothing else. There was an eerie silence. I hoped. I prayed. Nothing happened.

I waited. And waited.

Then something did happen. The nun responsible for my 'case' was suddenly beside me. She took my arm, more gently than the last time she had made physical contact with me.

'It's time, Nadia,' she said quietly.

No response.

'It's time, Nadia.' Her tone was more forceful. 'Come.' My whole body started to shake, and my legs felt like jelly as I was guided out of the room. I was reluctant to go willingly, but what good would it do to make a scene? They would probably question my sanity. But I was not insane. I was heartbroken. And there is a huge difference.

I did not want to leave my precious baby alone in this world without her mother to protect her. Back in the hostel, I hadn't been able to kill myself as a way for us both to be together. But I so wanted us to be together.

Over the past 14 days, I had felt suspended in time while arrangements were made for my baby's future. Now I felt completely numb. While I had been pregnant, there had still been hope. But my situation was now hopeless. All choice had been removed the moment I signed the form.

I had to sign to say I consented. But where did it cite 'under duress'? I re-read the form, but nowhere did it say that. I did, however, notice it said 'illegitimate' – meaning not legal – because my baby was born out of wedlock.

I only had one choice left. To draw a line under what had happened and move on with my life. But why did no-one understand it was not that simple? It was a baby's future which was being signed away? *My* baby.

Apparently, my travel arrangements had been made. I was to return to Ralf's house in London, then go back to Ceylon.

'Everything has been taken care of for you, to avoid minimum disruption,' said an emotionless nun. *How was it possible for a nun to be so clinical and detached?*

I'd thought perhaps Ralf might have had a change of heart and come to help me and little Mafalda. Instead, I was escorted with my few belongings to the front door of the big building. From the outside, it was a stunning building with an impressive entrance. It appeared inviting and grand, presenting the impression of somewhere warm and welcoming. But I had been inside for just over two weeks, and knew for certain that was simply an illusion.

There was no-one there to meet me. As the door closed behind me, I tried to make my way down the stairs with composure, but I stumbled slightly then quickly recovered.

The taxi driver was silent; he had obviously made this trip before. I sat in the back, alone in my thoughts all the way to the railway station.

The rest of the journey back to London was a blur. I remember nothing of it, and simply sat in a daze as the countryside whizzed past the grimy train windows.

When I'd spent time in the nursery with Mafalda, I'd heard some of the nuns use a sharp tone with the babies whose mothers had already been sent 'packing'. After some very traumatic births, many of the women had nothing to show but a fattened tummy and a heavy heart as they were physically evacuated from the building once they'd signed the papers for their babies to be adopted.

After one girl – Veronica – left, I heard a nun tell her baby, 'Your mother is not coming back. Accept it. If you don't, you will jeopardise your future, and no-one will want you.' Veronica's baby just cried as though she, too, was broken-hearted. The little one was inconsolable.

Now it was my turn to be sent on my way. *What would happen to my little Mafalda? Did she cry for me? Would she settle okay? Was she fed four-hourly? Did she miss my special words while having her nappy changed? Who would cuddle her?*

Chapter 24

Alone

I never went back to my family. From the station, I went straight back to the hostel, and used what little money I'd saved to start me off until I could claim national assistance again.

Once more, I was completely and utterly alone in a city I knew very little about. Like a zombie, lost in my misery, I walked round aimlessly for days on end, and slept very little. But I no longer prayed.

One day when I was out walking, I saw an advert for a job. I decided that if the job advert was still there the following day, I would apply for it. It was. I applied, and got the job.

Initially, I remained living in the hostel, but I gradually grew stronger and after a few months I rented a room.

It took me a long time to work out my new role in a society which had previously excluded me for being unmarried and pregnant. But I continued to work hard, and my professional life became my main focus. I was a classic example of someone who was 'married to the job'.

As time went on, there were a few men who invited me out on a dinner date or to go to the cinema after work, but I always declined. Eventually, they stopped asking.

However, several years after my loss, there was this one young man who I really liked. We went out a few times, and he was kind, friendly, and made me laugh.

We dated for a while but then I took cold feet. I got frightened and knew he would never accept me if I disclosed anything about my past and the situation I'd been in. But I could not live a lie by never telling him about the one thing that had changed my life so drastically. I would not take that risk. So I finished the relationship, telling him that I did not think it would work between us.

He pleaded with me, and even showed up a few times after I finished work. On one occasion he brought me a special gift from one of the big department stores – wrapped in tissue paper, boxed, and with a satin ribbon tied round the box. In those days, this suggested something very significant; it was a token of love. But after a few months, he finally gave up and stopped pursuing me. I was sad, but not as sad as I felt about giving up Mafalda.

I have only had two jobs in my working life. The first was as a secretary, which I was lucky to get. I had to bend the truth a little to get it, though. It was well known that when you lived in the hostel, your chances of changing the course of your life from negative to positive was very difficult. People judged you if you lived there, and appeared to have less respect for you as a human being. I don't know why.

So, I used Ralf and Kavindi's address when I provided my details, and hoped no-one would find out. But I did wonder sometimes if the boss knew I had lied.

I worked hard, became an established secretary at the company, and was friendly with colleagues, though not over-friendly. When they asked about my family, I would think of little Mafalda, and struggle not to burst into tears. I learned to excuse myself at those times, and go to the ladies' room where I could openly cry for my losses. Then, regaining my composure, I would return to my desk and continue working. The boss and my co-workers quickly stopped asking me anything personal.

One day, the boss asked me into his office and asked me where I lived. By then, thankfully, I had rented a flat and could give my true address. But I felt uncomfortable when he made eye contact, as though he knew I had lied.

He said, 'I have been wondering about you, Nadia. Something doesn't weigh up, but I can't put my finger on it. You're a strange one. I can't explain it, but I just felt when I interviewed you that I wanted to give you a chance to prove yourself.'

I felt my stomach lurch as I wondered what was coming. *Was I going to lose my job? Would I have to give up my flat and go back to the hostel?* I felt my eyes widen, and I knew I looked frightened.

But he smiled and said more gently, 'Relax, Nadia. You're a hard worker, and I would like to offer you a promotion.'

It was my turn to smile.

'I take it that is a yes?' he laughed.

'Yes, and thank you, Mr Diamond,' I replied.

'Well done, you have really impressed the management with your knowledge and capabilities. We don't want to lose you.'

I stayed faithful to that company for some time. After all, Mr Diamond had given me a chance and I felt I owed him some loyalty. He was a true gem, and we became good friends professionally.

He had been very kind to me, but he never questioned me again about anything related to my personal life. For that, I truly respected him. Some years later, I saw and then secured a job related to my social policy qualifications, and it was with genuine regret that I handed in my resignation. Mr Diamond accepted my resignation but said he was sorry to lose me. He also assured me that he would reemploy me anytime in the future, if I should require it.

On the day before I was due to leave, he invited me into his office for an off-the-record chat.

'You have a job here any time, Nadia, do you hear me?' he said.

'Yes, thank you, Mr Diamond.'

'I mean it, Nadia. You come and see me any time if things don't work out in your new job. I don't want to see you ever having to go back to the hard beginning you endured when you first started.'

I looked him straight in the eye, realising he probably had known all along that I had hidden my background and original address. But he smiled back, and I told him I would never forget his kindness and discretion.

I have never forgotten that day, nor the man who helped me on the road to professional success. He was a man of great intelligence, and he had shown great integrity. From that moment on, I strived to be the kind of role model he had been to me; it was something I tried to carry throughout my working life.

Chapter 25

Zoe Maria Anderson

Little Mafalda was given a new name once her adoption was finally completed. Zoe – meaning new life; Maria – according to the Catholic faith, after the Virgin Mother of God; and Anderson –her new family's surname.

She had lived in a children's home for some time, in the hope that a Catholic couple would adopt her. But couples tended to want small babies, not young children, and it was not easy to blend a Ceylonese baby into a family. The social workers knew that Mafalda was not going to be an easy child to place for adoption, so it was decided she would have to be moved to a unit for older children in the north of England. Luckily for her, a kindly nurse in the home became fond of her and interacted with the little one during her time there.

Once Sam and Maria accepted that they were unable to have a child of their own, they wasted no time in applying to adopt. They agreed that they would consider an older baby, if necessary.

After several months, and many interviews, the social worker told them about Mafalda, and they went to visit her at the home. From the minute they set eyes on her, they wanted 'Zoe' to be their first – and eldest – child.

Like all young children, she took a little while to settle, but Sam and Maria were determined to help her in every way. The social worker had told them that there was a strong Portuguese connection in Zoe's background, as Ceylon had a strong Portuguese influence.

Before she finally arrived to live with them, they travelled to one of the large department stores in the city to buy the best of bedding for her little cot. Immediately, Maria found herself drawn to a beautiful baby cover. She did not know why, yet when she touched it she noticed that the label said it was a Portuguese easy-care, satin-bound cover. Somehow, that felt comforting, in a strange way.

While tempted for a second to succumb to the traditional 'rose pink' for a girl, she resisted and bought cream instead. Maria knew that if all went well, Zoe would not be an only child. So, in her usual way, she reckoned that cream bedding would wash well and could be re-used for a boy or girl in the future.

'Sam, please can you come here?" she called across the store. 'Feel that. Do you like it?'

'Yes, why?

'Sam, it says on the label it's a Portuguese, easy-care, satin baby blanket.' She stopped when she saw his mystified look. 'Don't you remember the social worker talking about Zoe's heritage?'

'May I be of assistance to you?' a smiling shop assistant approached.

'Oh yes, please. We are going to require a cream one of these, and do you have any other Portuguese cotton items?' replied Maria enthusiastically.

'Madam, are you aware how expensive they are?' the assistant asked quietly.

'Oh yes.' Maria's eyes shone with excitement. 'But it's fine. We have been saving so hard for this day.'

'Well, if you follow me, we have this decorative pillow which is embossed using a skill still used in Portugal today, and which has been used for years and years. This *matelassé* finish is so beautiful. Look at the detail. You can see it has been hand-stitched.'

The all-over floral pattern was plain and simple, yet the effect was stunning. The shop assistant was smiling broadly, probably thinking about the potential sale.

'Yes, I can see that,' Maria agreed. 'It feels and looks lovely. What do you think, Sam, shall we take one?'

'Yes.'

'Do you have any cotton sheets to complement this set?' Maria turned her attention back to the assistant.

'Of course, madam, I'll show you the range. Your cot will be beautiful, like the girl or boy you are having.'

To Maria's surprise, Sam answered proudly, 'Yes, she's a beautiful little girl actually. We are adopting her, and she will be with us next week.' His wife was taken aback at such an overt public display of emotion to a virtual stranger.

But they both knew this display of apparent affluence would not last. Even though Sam was well paid in the factory, earning around £650 per annum, they had no intention of 'spoiling' their children with material goods. With love definitely, but never materially.

On the train heading home, they chatted with anticipation about the love which would fill every room now that their family was finally coming together. Truth be told, it was Maria who was chattering; Sam was listening, and occasionally adding the odd, 'Mm, yes of course, Maria.'

At one point, Sam glanced over at his wife and saw she was staring out of the window.

'Are you okay?' His voice was full of concern.

When she turned to face him, her eyes were brimming with tears, and his stomach lurched.

'What's wrong? Are you okay?' he asked again, leaning forward to touch her hand.

'Yes,' she murmured. 'I just can't believe it's really happening, can you?'

He squeezed her fingers gently and smiled. In his heart he knew that the darkest time of their lives was well and truly behind them. Family life would have many ups and downs, but he was sure they would handle it; they were strong, and they were a team. They would work through any problems together.

They had struggled through those dark days, but a bright light of hope and happiness had shone from within them both since the day the adoption officer told them about Zoe. A brightness so spectacular that even the Northern Lights would pale into insignificance.

Chapter 26

Mafalda? Zoe? One and the same

One night, after little Zoe had gone to sleep, Maria told Sam how incredibly lucky she felt that they finally had their daughter.

'But what if we hadn't adopted her?' she asked sadly. 'She might have ended up staying in the care system. Sam, what about all the other children who haven't been adopted, for whatever reasons?'

Sam nodded. 'Yes, there could well be other children lost in the care system due to their ethnicity. It must certainly have been a barrier in Zoe's case, as well as the stipulation that she was to be brought up Catholic.' He frowned, unable to hide his annoyance. 'What was her mother thinking about, making such a stipulation?'

***

Hundreds of miles away, in London, Nadia sinks wearily on to her settee, tired after a long, busy day at work. Her thoughts, as always, immediately turn to Mafalda and the other children like her, who have been denied their mothers purely on the grounds of being illegitimate.

'They broke me, and I have never felt complete since,' she muses. 'I am still heartbroken to have had to give her up for adoption. To be an outcast from society, and my family reject me. Will I ever get over it? Will I ever be rid of this aching hole inside me, which has become my darkest secret?'

She tries to lighten her mood and gets up to make herself a hot drink. As the kettle is boiling, she thinks of how she must appear on the surface to others, as a woman who is hard-working but quiet and often deep in thought, particularly on the 15th November each year. If only they knew that there was so much more to her story.

No doubt, some women might have shrugged off their mistake in the eyes of the Church, and married and moved on with their lives. Or did others, like me, take up a profession? What about the other lost souls wandering round, scanning every person in a crowd, hoping to catch a glance of their loved one. How are they dealing with the scars left behind?

She sighs and pours the boiling water into her cup. As the years have passed, she has come to understand that dealing with such a traumatic experience is very much an individual thing.

I hope my baby has had a good life. I really do. I hope she did not feel the impact of my sin. I have accepted that it is something which I carry with me all the time. On a daily basis, it is a fleeting thought, but every November 15, that pain becomes acute and almost unbearable.

Chapter 27

Zoe

Zoe had a good life with Sam and Maria. She settled well and loved her mum and dad −except, except perhaps, like many youngsters, during her teenage years. She also became the eldest daughter, when Sam and Maria went on to adopt three other girls to complete their loving and happy family.

Now married with children of her own, she has often thought how lucky she was to have had such supportive and loving parents. In her cosy kitchen in Scotland, she takes a welcome break from another hectic day of work and family life. She goes to the fridge, lifts out a bar of chocolate, takes one square, scoffs it quickly, then breaks off another three. The action reminds her of Sam, and she smiles as she remembers her mum complaining about how he would happily demolish a whole bar in one sitting.

Her father is like no other man she knows. He was of eastern descent but was Catholic. Yet, how was this possible when he hailed from the east coast of Scotland? No-one in the family knows why. Luckily for Zoe, he met the criteria stipulated for her adoption.

She remembers how he looked after her and her little sisters when their mother was ill and taken into hospital for months, declining the opportunity to put the family into temporary care until Maria recovered. He was adamant that he would manage one way or another – and he did.

Memories return of a conversation she once had growing up, when she asked Maria to tell her what it was like when they brought her to live with them.

'Well, we used to both get up at night if you cried. Once you settled again, we would stand and look at you sleeping in your cot. We couldn't believe our luck,' Maria told her. 'Your dad had to look after you and the others when I was ill and in hospital for six months. That wasn't easy, Zoe, because in those days men were workers, and childcare and working did not go hand-in-hand. But he refused to have you all put into care, as he did not want you to be any more unsettled. He can be stubborn and frustrating at times, your dad, but thank goodness he was stubborn on that occasion.'

Zoe recalls snatches of memories of her childhood, how her mother cared for each and every one of them, and how her dad helped with the washing, cleaning, and cooking, and showed them all love. He hadn't played as active a role domestically when the girls got older, mainly because his work took more and more of his time, but he had still enjoyed making dinner for the whole family at weekends.

As an adult with her own family, she can see clearly now what good role models her parents were, always striving for fairness and justice for all. Growing up, Zoe and her sisters had regularly fought and argued, falling out then falling back in, all growing as individuals at different rates.

She pops another square of chocolate into her mouth as she muses, 'We did appear to have a perfect childhood. We were very happy, safe, and loved. A proper family.

Should family games come with a warning label? she wonders.

Definitely. Memories of playing Monopoly – the areas of London so clearly detailed on the board; the pretend money; how good it felt to gather the £200 for passing 'Go', how frustrating it was if you landed on the 'Go to jail' space and had to pay the £50 to get out. Not to mention the fights before the game even started: who was getting the dog, the iron, the car, or even the ship. Was it all families who did that, or just hers?

But Maria and Sam, exchanging brief glances, would take a deep breath and ignore the squabbling, encouraging their daughters to get the game underway. Then they were off, and you could hear a pin drop as Susan counted out and organised the money, Lauren sat patiently, looking and planning what she was going to purchase, and Jennifer waited patiently for her turn. And it wasn't long before the peace was shattered.

How many times did we fight and argue? There always seemed to be someone leaving the game unfinished as they ran out of the room crying, 'That's not fair. I'm not playing any more!'

And it was the same when they played Cluedo, where the same pattern of events unfolded, fighting over Miss Scarlett or Professor Plum.

Then there was the game where they all put their hands on top of each other, then had to remove one hand and put it on top, and so on, until eventually it became quicker and quicker, with everyone pulling their hands out. It always ended in laughter.

Zoe reminisces at the pleasure she got watching her dad in awe as he peeled an apple, starting at the top and continuing until the skin came off unbroken. She had been so impressed, and desperate to be able to do it herself someday. *Ah, the simple things in life some children aspire to.* She smiles as the warm chocolate melts in her mouth.

Mum was such a great influence in our lives, too, she remembers.

Maria made a lot of her daughters' clothes, buying patterns and material from Remnant Kings, including the play trousers they all wore. They were complemented by the Ladybird T-shirts and, of course, the famous plastic sandals, which Zoe hated. Their mother had always been adamant that they had to change into their play clothes and out of their uniforms whenever they got home from school.

She suddenly has a flashback of them all going into Woolworths – a chain of nationwide stores, known as a one-stop shop – where you could buy pretty notepaper and pens to write letters to family back home, or a quarter of sweeties from the 'pick 'n' mix' as a Saturday treat, which they would enjoy that evening watching *The Generation Game* on TV.

The girls were always encouraged to update the family back in the east coast of any news, and in return they regularly received a copy of the local newspaper, with a brown address label wrapped around the rolled-up edition. It was always a highlight for Sam and Maria, as they discussed the local news in detail, and talked about the many people they seemed to know.

Maria always had a selection of ribbons for the girls' hair. These ribbons were washed, ironed, and put back in when they wore 'bunches' – a pony tail at either side of the head. Then there was the collection of buttons – large, small, detailed, in a variety of colours – sitting beside threads in bold and vibrant colours, chosen to exactly match the scarlet red corduroy, so that the stitching blended with the material to perfection.

Zoe smiles as she recalls her mum working on her much-treasured sewing machine, which had belonged to Maria's mother. She would describe herself jokingly as a 'make and mend queen', and would often laugh as she'd explain to Zoe about all the alterations she was going to make to an item before she would wear it. 'It will be fine once you take the buttons off, put in a zip, change the collar,' she'd say. 'it will be like a new top/dress.'

When she first had her own family, Zoe had been keen to be like her mother and become a homemaker. In the 1970s that had meant soaking all the white socks in the sink, then scrubbing them all by hand to ensure they were dazzling white. Women then often spent the whole day washing, using the boiler for cotton items and the sink for the other items, handwashing everything before spinning them in the spin-dryer. Thankfully, washing machines had taken over most of the job when it was Zoe's turn to care for her children's clothes.

But Zoe and her husband needed both their wages to secure a mortgage, so reluctantly she had gone back to work and relied on childcare.

She would love to be at home for her children, baking weekly – as Maria had done, making fairy cakes which had different toppings on them, as a treat for after tea.

'Please, can I just have one? I promise I will eat all my tea,' Zoe had often begged.

'No, proper nourishment first,' would be the stern reply. Of course, after tea she did get one.

Zoe wonders if her sisters have good memories of growing up, as well as the ones where they'd fought over toys and other issues.

As the eldest, Zoe had found it difficult at times, particularly in situations where she was the only child from a different origin. At times it had made her feel insecure in certain situations, but she'd never discussed it because she had nothing to compare it to. It had been hurtful, though, when other children had called her names purely because of her ethnicity.

At home, her role in the family had always been to look after the younger ones. And initially, she'd revelled in the power she'd thought it brought her, before being quickly reminded by her parents that she had to be a role model, showing care and compassion to her sisters.

Chapter 28

The magic of Christmas

Now that they were all adults, Zoe and her sisters had often spent hours at family get-togethers reminiscing about their childhood.

'I loved Christmas,' Zoe told the others, when they'd all been together recently. 'Even though it wasn't long after my birthday, Mum and Dad always made it such a special event.'

'I remember the night before Christmas, after saying prayers, we would hang up our stockings at the end of the beds, believing Santa would fill them once we were asleep,' Jennifer laughed.

'And he always did,' added Lauren, with a twinkle in her eyes. 'I loved the excitement in the morning when you couldn't wait to find out what was in it – an apple, or an orange, chocolate coins, maybe even a torch.'

It was Zoe's turn to laugh. 'Then we would go downstairs together into the living room, where there was a Santa sack for each of us with our name on it. It was the size and shape of a potato sack, the only difference being it was made of paper. And inside there were presents. Remember? Selection boxes, lots of chocolate bars – the ones we always had to hide from Dad!'

Jennifer joined in. 'I remember planning in which order I was going to eat the contents, it was such a treat.'

'Oh no, don't tell the story of the Flake again,' Zoe interrupted. 'We all know you pinched it!'

'I wasn't going to tell it again,' Jennifer huffed. Then she laughed at another memory. 'Remember one year there was a pretty peach bottle of hand and body cream. It had an ornamental peach for the lid, and I remember thinking this was a great gift to get, so I kept it for special occasions. And I loved getting the *Jackie* annual because it had all the photos and gossip about pop stars.'

'My best present was when I got a toytown post office set once. I was so thrilled at the notepaper, envelopes, stamps, even a stamp and a rubber ink pad. Remember, we played at post offices for hours?' Her sisters nodded at Susan's words. 'And then there was the time you got a mini projector, Lauren, which had slides in the form of a circle.'

'Yes,' added her eldest sister, 'it was slotted into the side of the projector. And I showed you how to use that, along with the light, to have "film shows" with the pictures projected onto the wall. We sat on the stairs and watched it, as if we were at the movies.'

'You even made tickets, which we had to use to get on to the stairs before any show could start,' Lauren chipped in. '"No ticket, no show," you always said.'

'Remember when I got a Bay City Rollers' V-neck jumper, which was contrasted in pink and black?' Zoe asked the others, warming to the theme. 'Half the sleeves and body were pink, and the other half black, and there was a black ribbed edge round the V. I was *so* chuffed with it! It took me ages to get ready for church that Christmas morning, because I couldn't make up my mind what to wear. I had all my new clothes I'd been given for Christmas, and I'd spent my birthday money the month before on a pair of black turn-up trousers, which

I'd saved to wear on Christmas Day.' She looked at her young-est sister. 'You probably won't remember the shop, Jen, but I bought them in the Skirt and Slack Centre in town, which sold school and fashionable clothes.'

Jennifer shook her head. 'No, it must have shut down before I got to the stage of buying clothes.'

'I remember Dad getting frustrated at how long it took me to get ready that Christmas morning,' Zoe giggled.

'I certainly remember you trying to wear make-up to school,' Lauren added. 'Poor Dad, having to listen to us argu-ing and discussing lip gloss and mascara every morning.'

'Ah, he loved it really,' suggested Zoe. 'There was one time I tried to put on the blue and green powder eyeshadow I'd saved so hard to buy. I rubbed one colour on my eyelid and the other one below my eyebrow, and thought I looked amaz-ing. But as I proudly walked towards the front door to go to school, I was gently reminded by Dad to "Get that muck off your face!" I told him it wasn't muck; it was the latest fashion. But he wasn't having any of it.'

'Mum was a bit more understanding about make-up and fashion, though, wasn't she?' asked Jennifer.

'Yes, I overheard her singing Donny Osmond's song *Young Love* one day, and couldn't understand how she could possibly know the words,' Zoe told them. 'But she just laughed and said that some Radio 2 DJ – Jimmy Young, I think – had had the same song in the hit parade a few years earlier. I didn't even know there was a Radio 2!' They all laughed.

'We had some great summer holidays, too, didn't we?' Lauren said wistfully. 'The weather always seemed perfect during the summer holidays from school back then.' Her sisters nodded. 'And I loved it when Mum had our tea made in a picnic-style, and then we'd go to the park when Dad came

home from work, and play outdoor games like rounders or...'
She suddenly has another memory. 'Oh, remember when we
got Tobermory tatties from the caravan park shop with our
holiday pocket money?'

'Even though it was happy at home, it was hard at times.'
Jennifer's tone became more serious. 'Having our own difficulties with our ethnic identities wasn't always easy. And we weren't
treated well at times by people who viewed us as different.'

'That's true,' Zoe agreed, but I have always strongly iden-
tified with my Scottish culture rather than my ethnic origin.
In all honesty, I've never had any desire to explore Ceylon in
any depth.'

'That was your experience, Zoe,' Lauren told her. 'Mine
was different.'

But Zoe wasn't to be deterred. 'I know you feel different,
Lauren, as we all do. But I feel that my life is the one I have
lived, rather than the one I could have lived. As a result, I
have never spent a lot of time wondering: what if I hadn't
been adopted? Because I was. Or what if I had been brought
up in the care system? Because I wasn't. I became Mum
and Dad's eldest daughter,' she paused to smile at Jennifer,
Lauren and Susan, 'and your big sister. And that will always
be my response.'

Chapter 29

Zoe: Why the colourful butterfly?

I can only ever imagine the pain my natural mother would have suffered in giving me up for adoption. I am acutely aware of this, and feel great empathy for her. But I am also aware that my adoption has been a positive one, so perhaps that is the main reason I would not look into my background any further. I meant what I said to my sisters that day.

But I have spoken about it many times to my mum, Maria, over the years. I remember that there had been an element of teenage curiosity, when I'd wondered who I looked like. But the thought passed as quickly as the teenage years.

'I have no desire to go Sri Lanka on holiday,' I once told her, 'but I do wonder sometimes why I love such bold and vibrant colours.'

Mum had nodded in understanding. 'I did notice that as your confidence developed, so did your ability to wear bright colours with ease. You were like a magnet to them.' She laughed. 'Even with something as simple as 'Trophy' Basmati rice, which was in a plum and fuchsia pink packet, with an embossed gold pattern. You always seemed to choose it over the blue and white packet sitting beside it on the shelf in the supermarket.

'As your life progressed through the years, you became a woman in your own right. And I am so happy for the choices that were available to your generation but were denied to many women previously. I feel great sadness for the many women who had their babies so tragically taken from them in those days. My life has had its ups and downs, but nothing compared to the pain I imagine of having to forcibly give up your baby.' She had hugged me then before continuing. 'All in all, I think you and your sisters have had a good life growing up in our family.'

'We did, Mum.' I assured her, dropping a gentle kiss on her cheek. 'But then,' I teased, 'I have nothing to compare it to, do I?'

As I watched her smile fade a little, I added, 'Seriously, Mum, I don't remember anything of my early beginnings. My natural mother's family held the key to what I could have been. But you and Dad, Jennifer, Lauren, and Susan, all hold the key to who I became.'

Chapter 30

Serendipity?

Nadia pours herself another cup of tea from the pretty teapot, and stares unseeingly around the Cinnamon Café. *Will I ever meet her?* she wonders.

It's six weeks before the 15th November, and Nadia is sitting in her usual seat. She feels a little emotional today, but without the same intensity that usually comes with that special date. Today, the feeling is a fleeting pang, and she dabs her eyes gently with her handkerchief then puts it back in her pocket.

The café, as always, is busy. A young woman, in her late thirties perhaps, comes in and closes the door to shut out the chilly wind. She looks around for a seat and her eyes fall on the unoccupied one opposite Nadia.

'Hello, is there anyone sitting there?' the young woman asks politely.

'No.' Nadia shakes her head.

'Do you mind if I sit there?'

'Not at all,' Nadia replies, moving her teapot slightly to make space on the other side of the table. 'Please sit down.'

Glancing at the young woman as she takes off her light jacket and settles it behind her on the seat, Nadia is struck by her features. She is Ceylonese! Nadia can tell by the bone structure of the girl's face and her features, but she tries not to stare. She steals a few glances then turns her attention back to her cup of tea.

An overwhelming desire makes her want to look back, so this time she pretends to look at other customers beyond the woman, but is stunned at the similarity between them. *Is it purely ethnic?* Nadia isn't convinced. *It is like looking at a mirror image of me many years ago.* In fact, the young woman looks like a much younger mixture of her and Ralf. *How can this be possible?*

Nadia begins to feel a bit faint. Unsure whether it is the shock of this young woman's appearance or the humid atmosphere in the café, she sips her tea and tries desperately to regain her composure. But her mind is whirling, and she physically nips her arm to make sure she isn't dreaming. *Ouch! No, that hurt; I'm not dreaming.*

The young woman, catching Nadia's glance, smiles and starts to chat about the weather in a strong Scottish accent. *She appears oblivious to the striking resemblance between us*, Nadia realises. She cannot explain the rising feeling of emotion which is beginning to bubble under the surface of her skin. She is struggling to identify what the emotion is; her mind is a jumble of thoughts.

Just then, the café owner Sam Anderson approaches. 'Is that you trying to sneak in unnoticed?' he jokes.

The young woman turns to him with a beaming smile. 'Oh Dad, I wanted to sit and observe you hard at work, I thought I would have had a little longer before you spotted me. It's been a long day.' She stands up and they hug each other. 'I'm glad to be here at last, instead of you always coming to me.'

'Is everyone okay at home?' he asks.

'Yes,' his daughter assures him. 'The bairns will be well looked after by their dad.' She crosses her fingers and they both laugh.

Sam shakes his head. 'Another dad left as head cook and bottle-washer, eh? I'll bet they will have more fun without you.'

The young woman lands a playful punch on his arm. 'Aw, Dad, stop it. My first time leaving them was always going to be hard.'

He claps a hand on her shoulder to reassure her. 'They'll be fine, Zoe.' His face brightens. 'Your mum will be back soon. She's just gone on an errand.'

'No problem. My train was a bit early getting in.'

'Do you want to go upstairs?' he asks.

'No, Dad, I'm fine here.' She sits back down. 'I'll sit here and watch the master at work.'

He laughs. 'Right then, what can I get you?'

'Oh, just a tea. I had something to eat on the train.'

'Any brand do? Or would madam like something more specific?' he jokes.

'A good strong cup of Ceylonese tea, please, and don't forget to bill me. I want mates' rates; or family rates will do nicely.'

Surreptitiously listening to the conversation, Nadia almost gasps when she hears the woman's choice of tea.

'And what does that mean?' Sam looks confused.

'Oh, you know, I'll wash the dishes until my debt is paid in full. But I can't stay too long.'

Nadia realises this must be some kind of private joke, which they have obviously shared many times before.

While she watches this exchange, Nadia's mind is struggling to comprehend what's going on. *It just can't be. How could this be possible? Oh God, have you really made our paths cross again? is this the moment I have waited almost 40 years for?*

Sam leaves to get his daughter's order and Zoe turns towards Nadia with an apologetic smile. She then focuses on her mobile phone, and taps out a text before her father places her tea on the table along with a wholemeal scone and honey.

The young woman seems to sense Nadia's gaze. 'Do you come here often?' she asks.

'Yes,' Nadia manages to reply, her mouth dry. 'I like this café.'

The girl nods as she spreads honey on her scone. 'Me, too.' A comfortable silence settles between them as she focuses on her scone and pours her tea.

Nadia desperately tries to process what's going on. *It can't be Mafalda; but she has just ordered my favourite order. How is this possible? Coincidence?* Then she shakes her head at her train of thought. *Stop being so stupid*, she tells herself. *The woman has only ordered a scone and tea.*

The young woman picks up the conversation again. 'You know, this is my mum and dad's café, but it's actually the first time I have managed to visit.' She smiles and looks around the room proudly. 'I am so happy for them. It was a pipe-dream which they turned into a reality.'

'Really?' Nadia feels as though she is holding her breath.

'Yes. I am so very proud of them. It's usually the other way around,' she chuckles. 'Normally, the parents are proud of their children's achievements.' She sips her tea briefly. 'I live in Scotland, so I've been trying to come down for some time, but never seem to make it, what with family life and work.'

Chapter 31

Do it, don't dream

'Zoe!' A woman's voice calls across the café. 'I'm sorry I wasn't here when you arrived.'

'Hi Mum.' Zoe gets up wearily to hug her mother. She is tired from the journey, and still a little anxious about how her husband and children will cope while she is away.

Her mother is clearly excited to see her. 'Now then, let's get you upstairs.'

Zoe takes her jacket off the back of the chair and lifts her bag, stopping briefly to smile and say goodbye to the pleasant woman sitting opposite her. Although she is delighted to see her mum, she would have liked to sit and chat to the woman a little longer.

Later that evening, after the café is closed and they have enjoyed one of her mum's delicious meals, Maria asks, 'Are you any further forward with your book?'

Zoe shrugs and shakes her head. 'Mum, I just don't have time.'

It has been Zoe's dream since childhood to write a book, and she has already started and stopped many times, only to put it aside again.

She has been so busy with the children and work that she hasn't had a chance to visit her parents since they moved to

London to open the café. But her husband had encouraged her to come; he felt it would help her with her book.

When she'd received the information in her adoption file, she and her parents had been stunned to find out that her birth mother had been living in a homeless unit not far from the Cinnamon Café. *Why was she there? Did she have no family?* Zoe had felt so sad for her mother; it must have been so hard to live in a homeless unit in 1960, alone, and pregnant. *Why was she there?* The paperwork said her family had given a car and £6000 pounds to get rid of the young boy who got her pregnant. The typed letter, which Zoe had thought was strange, had been given to her while other information in her file had been held back to protect a third party. Zoe could only presume that the stipulation to keep the information secret had been paid for by someone desperate to remove all traces of the baby's history.

Once Sam has kissed them both goodnight and headed off to bed, Zoe and her mum chat into the small hours about the information Zoe has discovered about her early beginnings. And they are both tearful as they discuss how hard it must have been for her natural mother to give up Zoe.

'You do know I love you and Dad,' Zoe tells Maria. Although she is curious about her birth, she is conscious that she doesn't want to hurt the loving parents who brought her up.

'Of course we do,' replies Maria. 'Now, come on, you must be tired. Get to bed and we can chat more tomorrow.'

For some reason, Zoe can't stop thinking about her encounter with the woman in the café today. She had felt drawn to her; there had been something comforting about the woman. *Maybe lots of people in London are like that*, she tells herself.

As they head up the stairs, she asks her mum, 'Did you see that woman I was sitting with in the café today when you came in?'

Maria thinks briefly then shakes her head. 'No,' she replies. 'Why?'

Zoe shrugs. 'I don't know. There was just something about her I liked.'

Chapter 32

No, it can't be!

The next day at lunchtime, Nadia is back in the Cinnamon Café after a restless night in which her mind had churned with memories and possibilities. Since their meeting, she has been unable to forget the young woman's beaming smile and how it lights her eyes and her whole face.

If only I didn't have an important appointment to keep this afternoon, I could stay and maybe catch another glimpse of her. But I can't postpone it.

Nadia asks for the bill and goes to the counter to pay. She feels a strong emotional connection with this young woman who is the proprietor's daughter, and she wonders whether she should question him.

She believes in her head and in her heart that this girl Zoe could be her Mafalda, but she doesn't know how to find out. How can she broach the subject with Sam, to find out if their daughter is adopted? And if she is, they might not want her to meet her natural mother and bridge the gap between them after all these years.

Maybe I could just approach Zoe? she thinks, then dismisses the idea. *That would be selfish.*

As she leaves the café, Nadia wonders if Sam and his wife have ever thought about her own ethnicity, or noticed her striking resemblance to their daughter? *Surely they must see it?*

She mulls over and over in her head how best to act. *I have to really work this one out with the precision of a heart surgeon performing a lifesaving operation. If I make the slightest error, I could cause more harm than good. I must not be rash. I must have faith. If God has forgiven me and put my Mafalda back in my path, then he will surely guide me to the correct decision.* For the first time in many years, Nadia thinks she will pray tonight.

***

The following day, Nadia is still unnerved by the chance encounter with Zoe. November 15 is only weeks away, and for some reason this year she feels more overwhelmed by emotion. Her heart hurts almost as badly as it did on that fateful day she had to leave her little Mafalda in the home.

Although it is lunchtime, she manages to sit at her usual table, and takes a deep breath to try to relax as she sees Sam approach to take her order. But her mind is in turmoil. *Say it now: Ask him about his daughter,* says one voice. But another voice in her head tells her: *Don't be so stupid. What will you say? I'm Nadia, I think I am your daughter's natural mother. You know, the one who left her in the mother and baby home. Oh, and don't forget my parents wanted her brought up Catholic.*

As he walks away with her food order, she feels the tears prick at the back of her eyes. But she is angry at herself for her public display of emotion, and quickly regains her composure. As she waits, she links her feelings to that of a volcano, which has been bubbling at the earth's core over many, many years, and as the optimum conditions have now been reached she could explode. *But who knows what damage the eruption would have on the innocent bystanders who would be engulfed in the red-hot flames of my anger, spilling over and over, gaining momentum, and destroying everything in its path?*

She waits for what feels like an eternity for her order. But when it comes, Nadia feels sick. She cannot eat or drink a

145

thing. She looks at her watch, then goes to the counter and asks for the bill. She pays with her debit card, as usual, then leaves. Nadia walks and walks and walks. She finds herself in Kew Gardens, and sits down on an empty bench, oblivious to the noise and chatter of the many visitors. Today, she can't even contemplate the broad walk from palm house to the Orangery and round the corner to the main gate. Normally, she loves the tranquillity associated with the Azalea Garden, the Palm House, and the Rose Garden. She knows this road so well that she could navigate it from memory, but today she feels disorientated.

She remembers walking and walking when she first came to London. She'd walked aimlessly for hours and hours with nowhere to go and unable to return to the hostel till evening, so she'd come to Kew Gardens and pass some time. *Despite my sadness, I was able to almost touch the tranquillity. The gentle movement of the trees reminded me so much of home.* She had found a bit of peace there at a time when her life was in such turmoil. Perhaps that's why she still always seemed to navigate here like a homing bird every time her emotional pain threatened to overwhelm her.

She remembers how at first she'd had to focus on something other than her pain, so she'd started reading all about the park. Its history once again comes back into her racing brain, and she takes a deep breath and sits quietly, allowing the snatches of information to wash over her.

Owned by the Earl of Essex's brother, Sir Henry Capel, before it came into Royal ownership in 1718, the park was visited by many royals over the years. Sir Joseph Banks, a botanist who sailed round the world with Captain James Cook, was appointed by the King to take charge of the gardens, and he encouraged plant hunters to search far and wide and send back exotic species from the West Indies, Africa, Australasia,

China, and India. She could almost recite the guidebook information after all these years.

On other days, when her pain was not so acute, she would go to the Palm House and observe the Cycad, labelled 'the oldest pot plant in the world', and which was brought back from Africa in 1775.

She remembers why this place became soothing at times of great pain. She has always felt it is like a living picture which brings her great comfort. Her favourite time has always been autumn, when the trees are shedding their leaves, and she can admire the contrasting vibrant colours – green, brown, yellow, red, and orange, fit enough for any king – against the crisp, deceiving chill.

As she tries to regain her composure, she recalls the many times she has watched the beautiful and vibrant spring daffodils. She used to see them moving gracefully from side to side, and imagine they were swaying and could carry her love so very far away, and hope that her Mafalda would catch that love wherever she was. *I know it was stupid, but it was the only thing I could think of at the time to try to mend my broken heart.*

She is reminded of the words of the poet Wordsworth:

> *For oft when on the couch I lie*
> *In vacant or in pensive mood*
> *They flash upon that inward eye*
> *Which is the bliss of solitude*
> *And then my heart with pleasure fills,*
> *And dances with the daffodils.*

This place was her saving grace when sadness was weighing down her heart, when she knew that her life would never be the same again.

Nadia sits deep in thought now. She is annoyed with herself. So many times, she has planned in her mind what she would say if she ever met her daughter again. A gust of wind disturbs her thoughts and she glances at her watch, thankful that she still has some time before her lunch break is over. On days like this, the company's flexi-time can help her to maintain a sense of normality to the outside world. If she needs a little longer, she knows she can always use some of the extensive extra time she devotes to doing her job. Her current boss, like Mr Diamond all those years ago, is very understanding.

Today, she acknowledges that she needs that extra time to regain her composure before going back to work.

She drifts back into her tortured thoughts. *Have I once again failed my little Mafalda?* She has wracked her brain trying to think how best to ask Sam about his daughter. She knows that it isn't in her character to open up to other people, but has hoped that she might manage to find the right words at the right time.

She checks her watch again, and becomes aware of how quickly time has passed. But she is still unsettled; the enormous emotional wedge she is trying to unblock from her heart won't shift. She desperately needs closure. She has been trying to get better with each passing year, but she still feels the physical pain in her heart.

No-one can understand, unless they have had their baby stolen from them. As November 15 approaches every year, no matter how hard she tries, she can't shift the aching in her heart… in her whole body.

Nadia puts her head in her hands, overwhelmed again by her emotions. She is usually so composed. She knows that once the anniversary has passed, she will once again manage to stuff those feelings back under the surface, where they will stay firmly in place until the next year.

She stands up and gives herself a mental and physical shake before heading back to her office. But despite her attempts to go about the rest of her day, she cannot shake off her uneasy feelings, and decides to finish early.

She feels even more unsettled by the time she goes to bed. *I have not prayed for such a long time. Should I have faith once more?* She ponders for some time, but after some deliberation chooses not to pray. *It did not help me at my most vulnerable time, so why would it work for me now?*

The pain is excruciating and seems much worse than usual this year. She sighs. *Could I have tried harder to keep my baby?* She shakes her head. She knows things were what they were, and it was such a long time ago now. She is weary at having to live with this secret for so long. Life feels difficult and very hard just now; she is overwhelmed with tiredness.

It feels like a lifetime ago that she thought she saw Mafalda, yet it was only a few days. She tries to concentrate, but feels so confused about that meeting in the café. *What actually happened? Why did it upset me so much? Was it Mafalda?*

Chapter 33

Head cook and bottle washer!

Zoe loves watching her dad at work in the café. He looks so calm and completely at ease with the customers. She feels so proud of her parents for realising their dream after all these years, and building up such a successful business; she can see how happy it makes them.

A wave of emotion rises in her and she feels her eyes beginning to smart. She and her sisters had suggested they bring in a manager to allow them some time to themselves, but her parents had insisted that you could not capture this atmosphere merely by hiring more help. And since she has been here, she has become more and more convinced that her parents' decision to resist was the right thing to do. However, Maria and Sam have finally decided to advertise for some help, but are determined to take their time to find the right person.

She knows by observing her dad how much he is in his element, as her mum says. And she's right. Zoe loves the feel of the café, its delicately subtle decoration and surroundings, and good, tasty food. And it is obvious that people enjoy the interaction with her parents.

Zoe wonders if they ever regret having their family; if they'd had no children, they could have pursued their dream when they were much younger. But her thoughts are interrupted by her mum coming into the café. Together, they head upstairs chatting and laughing, to prepare dinner.

'Was it always this perfect, Mum?' she asks.

'What do *you* think, Zoe?'

They look at each other and laugh. Of course it wasn't. They both remember the teenage tantrums, the fights with her sisters, so many different personalities all under one roof.

'Trials and tribulations can be exhausting,' Zoe admits.

But her mother just laughs. 'You seem very knowledgeable.'

Chapter 34

Ah, the simple pleasures!

The next day once they have finished work for the day and the café is closed, Sam, Maria, and Zoe head out to a local restaurant for dinner.

Over their meal, Zoe chats to them about her life, her family, and the changes which have happened since they were last together. Although they speak regularly by telephone, they miss the detail and expressions Zoe uses. When she is back home with her work commitments and family to look after, she doesn't have the same time to talk to them as in the old days.

Zoe misses having them live so close by, but she would never tell them that. She made a promise to herself not to make her parents feel guilty for pursuing their dreams. One of her friends was devastated when her parents wanted to emigrate and start a new life in Australia, and their children were so upset that the couple pulled out of their move, stayed in Scotland, and lost a lot of money on flights and accommodation. Yet only a few years later, one of the children moved to Canada, and the parents now split their time between the UK and Canada to try and keep up their family ties.

Zoe and her sisters use the internet, phone calls, and visits – usually by Mum and Dad – to keep their family ties strong.

She laughs when she remembers her mum being reluctant to use the internet instead of writing a letter.

'A letter on Basildon Bond paper and a first-class stamp was good enough for your dad and me when we moved away from our parents,' she'd complained at the time. 'Mark my words, writing letters will become fashionable again, and the price of the paper will be sky-high once all the young ones are hooked.'

'Oh Mum,' they'd laughed, 'don't be so cynical.'

But Maria had given in and slowly got used to the technology. Now she regularly emails her daughters, although she still isn't comfortable at trying to operate Skype.

Being together again, and catching up with all the news and reminiscing, has been wonderful for all three of them. Zoe's stay with her parents seems to have passed so quickly. And while she is sad to leave them, she is looking forward to getting home to her husband and children. Back to the routine of 'porridge and old clothes' – an old Scottish expression used to indicate a holiday is over and it's time to get back to normal routine.

***

The following morning, Zoe and her parents say their goodbyes amidst promises to phone and email, and Sam and Maria's plans to head north for Christmas.

Once Zoe is on the train, she texts her husband to let him know what time her train is due, then settles back in her seat and reflects on an enjoyable few days. She is only too aware how lucky she is to have been adopted by Sam and Maria. Her life could have been so very different, even if her natural mother had kept her.

Even now, as an adult and a mother herself, Zoe doesn't waste any time wondering 'what if?' Content and grateful with her life, she has always been a great believer that life is what it is, despite any ups and downs. Her passion for her job has never waned, and more importantly, her family life defines and completes her as a person.

She is a product of the 1960s' adoption system, but she is not bitter. She and her family have enjoyed a positive adoption experience, though she is aware that many others haven't.

As the motion of the train relaxes her, Zoe gives a fleeting thought to her natural mother's situation at that time. *What was she like, the woman who had me? I can never think of her as Mum. I wonder what her reason for was giving me up. Was she careless? Was she in love?* It was a different society then; a less forgiving one. Maybe one day I'll go to the adoption society and try to find out more. Maybe I will eventually write that book.

Zoe's thoughts drift back to her parents' café. She seemed to be drawn to one particular table during her visit, but she couldn't explain why. It was the strangest feeling. She remembers feeling unsettled and staring out of the window, then a shiver had gone down her spine and she'd suddenly felt colder. It hadn't upset her at the time, but now she realised it had been a bit creepy. It was if someone had walked over her grave.

Anyway, note to self, she smiles as she thinks, *just don't sit there again next time you visit.* Her thoughts are interrupted by the familiar sound of a text message on her phone.

She smiles as she reads the message, then quickly texts her reply:

Thanks, Mum, it was great. Love you both. Will miss you too. Lots and lots of love, Zxx

She feels the tears prickling behind her eyes. How she hates leaving them.

Chapter 35

Home is where the heart is

Today is different from every other November 15th, and Nadia doesn't know why. She can't explain it, but she just can't shake off the feeling.

As she makes her way to the counter of the Cinnamon Café to pay for her tea, she reaches into her pocket for a tissue, and at the same time pulls out a £5 note. *Where did that come from?* She must have slipped it into her pocket instead of putting it back in her office drawer to buy a mid-morning snack.

She approaches the counter and holds out the note, but as Sam takes the money, their hands touch. They briefly look into each other's eyes, both sending a strong emotional connection. She knows he felt it, too, as he appears to jump back as if embarrassed at the touch of their hands.

He starts chatting nervously in a way he has never done with her before. *Does he think she is interested in him and planning on asking him out on a date or something?*

'Do you know what date it is today?' he asks her.

Nadia's heart drops, and her mouth suddenly feels dry. 'Yes, I do,' she replies sadly, and lowers her eyes.

'A special day in our family. One I am so grateful for. It's my eldest daughter's fortieth birthday.'

***

Why am I so embarrassed? Why am I telling her this? thinks Sam. *I hardly know this woman.* But his mouth again seems to go into action before his brain is in gear.

'Oh, that's lovely for you,' Nadia replies, struggling to sound enthusiastic.

'Did you maybe see my daughter last week when you were in?' he asks. 'Zoe is visiting all the way from Scotland. We have four girls, actually. All adopted. Maria always says that being a parent is not about giving birth, it's so much more. I have always been the stubborn one, but she was so right. I have been privileged to be given the opportunity to become a father to my girls.' He laughs. '*Our* girls.'

The woman clears her throat. 'That's lovely,' she says again. 'I hope you were always happy.'

'Happy?' he chuckles. 'Have you ever been a parent?' She shakes her head. 'Happiness comes in waves when you have daughters.'

There is a brief pause before she speaks again. 'What are your daughters like? You seem very proud of them.'

'Yes, of course,' Sam replies proudly. The café is quiet at this time, so he has plenty of time to talk, and the awkwardness between them seems to have passed. 'As I said, our eldest daughter, Zoe, was born on the 15th November. She weighed just 5lbs 12oz. She was here last week visiting us from Scotland – that's where we come from originally. It's the first time she has managed to come down since we bought the café. She is so busy with her work and family.

'Maria always asks our girls to say a prayer for their natural mothers each year on their birthdays. And we have been blessed to have been given the privilege of loving and caring for them.' He searches her face to see if the woman is listening. She seems very thoughtful. 'Would you like to see a photograph of my girls?'

'Yes,' she replies quickly. 'I would be honoured.'

He pulls out his wallet and shows her a photograph of four young girls, smiling happily for the camera. Then he takes out another photograph – one of his wife and him on their wedding day.

Nadia stares in amazement. She is struck by how alike the young Sam in the photograph is to their oldest daughter, Zoe. But the little girl is also the exact image and mixture of both Ralf and her at that age. *Oh, it must be my Mafalda*, Nadia thinks. The girl looks so happy.

Sam observes a series of emotions flit across the face of the woman in front of him; he can't understand why she seems so moved. *Maybe it's because she doesn't have any children of her own*, he thinks. She's a good and regular customer, so he hopes he hasn't upset her.

Nadia tears her eyes away from the happy photograph and looks directly at him.

'Thank you,' she says, her voice much stronger now.

'Thank you?' he asks, puzzled.

'Yes. For everything.' Nadia smiles.

'Everything?'

She nods without saying any more. But so many thoughts are running through her head, and she feels the strangest sensation as her body begins to tingle. It starts deep in her chest, like a phoenix rising from the ashes, and her heart is beating faster. It is like an out-of-body experience, whereby she no longer feels like the Nadia she has become over the past 40 years.

Another customer appears at Nadia's shoulder to pay his bill.

'If you wait a minute, I'll tell you about the other three,' Sam says, smiling.

Nadia shakes her head and moves away from the counter. 'I'm sorry,' she says. 'I can't wait. I have an appointment. But thank you.'

He looks a little disappointed, but smiles back. 'My pleasure. Goodbye.'

'Goodbye.'

Chapter 36

Nadia

When I left the café, I knew I had found the key to slowly unlock my broken heart.

I am sure I have finally seen my Mafalda, yet the encounter was not as simple as I had hoped it would be. I had naively thought I would be different from all the other women I had heard about who met up with their adopted children. *But why would I, of all people, be so much more able to deal with this?*

I don't know which is better: the suppressed pain which has become a kind of familiarity to my life for the past forty years; or this new experience, which has inadvertently reopened a painful wound buried so deeply and 'neatly' compartmentalised to allow me to survive. It feels like a hole in my soul which I have never been able to close.

I have been unable to sleep properly. I have been crying constantly at home, behind closed doors. I can be watching TV then my eyes will well up and I find myself sobbing. I am completely confused by my emotions.

I have worked so very hard over the past forty years to compartmentalise my pain. After leaving the café today, I came home and tried to organise my thoughts. My heart was beating faster, I was sweating. I tried to calm myself using a breathing technique, but I began to wonder if my mind was playing tricks on me. Did I really see my Mafalda in the Cinnamon Café that day? Did I really have a bizarre conversation with Sam today, where he was telling me his daughter was born on the 15th November weighing 5lb 12oz, that he and his wife had adopted her? Has my Mafalda enjoyed a good life?

I am not going mad. I know I did not dream this up. After all, I have resigned myself for over forty years that I would never know what happened to my child.

I start to walk round my flat. I am completely agitated and confused by the overwhelming emotions I am experiencing. My brain cannot cope. *How is it possible that I could meet my Mafalda in the Cinnamon Café and even have had a conversation with her? Why this year of all years?*

Has God finally forgiven me, or is it that I have finally forgiven myself for my sin and the impact of that on my baby? I am so confused, I think I am going mad. I keep crying with the pain. I thought it would be easy to see my Mafalda and still be able to keep that part of my heart concealed, but I have found this almost as painful for a very different reason.

I know I can never be anything to my Mafalda; that was lost forever two weeks after her birth. But this searing pain in my heart is so painful. Meeting her has opened up the black hole which I thought I had managed to close. It feels as though I am suffocating in sadness and for the personal life I was never able to create. I lost everything that mattered to me all those years ago.

My work has filled the gap Monday to Friday over all that time. No-one knows that once I say goodbye to my co-workers and close my door on a Friday evening, I do not speak to anyone until the Monday morning when I return to work. The first person who speaks to me probably doesn't even notice that my lips make a kind of popping noise when I say good morning to them.

For so long, I have ached with all my being to know what happened to my Mafalda. That feeling has been my constant companion for over forty years. Having lost touch with all my family, my work became my main purpose in life. Whenever I was there, I was able to become completely focussed, and had a special way of being able to reach out to the clients I worked with. I knew my empathy for their individual situations gave me a great sense of purpose. The wall behind our desks is filled with photographs and thank you cards sent directly from the people themselves...

But I have felt different recently; I cannot explain why. I have been so tired. *Did I really meet Mafalda the other day? Did I have the most bizarre conversation with Sam today?*

With my thoughts still racing in my mind, I walk over to where I put my handbag and search frantically for the coins lying at the bottom. £2.45 – the change Sam gave me.

I never pay for things with cash; I always use my debit card. So, what made me lift the £5 note I normally keep in my drawer as emergency funds? Emergency funds? I smile as I think about this. For someone with my past to call it emergency funds is quite amusing. The emergency in this case is usually if I want to buy a bag of crisps or a bar of chocolate when I need an energy boost at work. I am not mad.

My brain is trying to register that I am actually finally happy. That my little Mafalda has had a good life. *Was it really with Sam, his wife, and their other girls?*

But I feel so very alone. I have such a longing to be back home, feeling safe and secure. I close my eyes and imagine in my mind that I am back at a cafe in Ceylon enjoying high tea, with a little girl looking up at me with a smile on her face. *Am*

I that little girl, perhaps in happier times? Or is it my little Mafalda? It no longer matters.

I get up again, still feeling so unsettled. I run a hot bath, pour myself a large Bacardi and Coke, and take a large bag of crisps with me. I don't normally overindulge, but today I am going to let my body have whatever it wants.

As I lie in the bath, I allow my mind to wander again while the comfort of the warm water swirls over my body. I feel the heat permeate into my very soul. I have waited so long to feel like this. The warmth I have been craving inside for so long, finally feels so good. I inhale with a sigh then breathe out, unaware I have been unconsciously holding my breath.

The searing pain starts again in my chest. I feel such a longing to be back in Ceylon, with all the family, sitting around the table. I close my eyes and visualise the homecoming of the 'prodigal' daughter. *Have they fattened a lamb? Will my father run to greet me, to tell me all is forgiven?*

The house smells familiar. The aroma of freshly made tea is strong. I observe the paintings on the wall. I visualise the cheerful dining room.

'Ah, there you are. Where were you, Nadia?' asks my mother.

'We have been looking for you?' says my father.

'I'm here,' I reply.

They both smile warmly, and I look around at the picture of perfection.

Suddenly, I begin to retch as if I am going to be sick. This distorted perception I am experiencing is heart-breaking. *Do they not know what they did to me?* Of course they don't. They did not care. I am still. I try to open my mouth. Nothing comes out. Never mind. Today is the first day of the rest of my life.

I feel warm. I feel relaxed. I feel a warm tear roll down my cheek. I feel my heart pumping like it's about to burst outside of my body. *Is this what it feels like to be complete? Or have I died, and certainly not gone to heaven?*

Chapter 37

The ultimate price

Sam and Maria are glancing through the local evening newspaper to check the advert they have placed looking for staff to help over the festive period. As Sam turns one of the pages, they spot the photograph of a woman.

'Can I see that a little closer, Maria?' Sam takes the paper from her.

'You look like you have just seen a ghost,' she tells him.

'I have. This is the woman who comes into the café.' He points to the photograph.

'Yes, I thought that,' she replies. 'I am as shocked as you.'

He shakes his head. 'No, Maria, you don't understand. I had the most bizarre experience last week, but I forgot to tell you. I spoke to this woman last week, but I got into such a state. It was such a strange encounter.'

'What encounter?' Maria is confused. 'Sam, you're making no sense.'

'It was on Zoe's birthday. For some reason, I ended up telling that woman in the paper about our girls.'

'What about them?' Maria is growing frustrated.

'When she came to pay her bill, our hands touched, and it was strange. It was not anything I had ever experienced before, Maria.' He frowns and runs his hand through his hair in exasperation. 'I can't explain it. It wasn't romantic or anything. I don't know why I got embarrassed, but I just started rambling.'

Maria smiles fondly. 'Well, you do tend to ramble.'

'No, this was different,' he says. 'I ended up telling her about you, me, the girls. I even showed her the photographs I keep in my wallet. Now that I come to think about it, I never told her about the girls. I only managed to tell her about Zoe, because someone came to the counter, and when I was about to tell her about the other girls she said she had to leave.

'But she seemed so sad when I told her it was Zoe's birthday,' he muses, trying to remember their conversation. 'I felt so bad because she said she didn't have any children.'

'Who was she?' Maria is intrigued. 'What does the newspaper say?'

Together they read the obituary article next to the photograph of charity worker, Dr Nadia Selon – the woman who had visited their cafe so many times over the years.

Dr Selon was a dedicated and passionate employee of a charity helping adopted children to be reconnected with their natural mothers. One of her co-workers, Veronica Taylor, told the Gazette: *'Nadia loved her work, and she will be sorely missed. She dedicated over thirty-five years to the organisation, and carried out her duties with great care, compassion, and diligence.'*

Dr Selon, who was unmarried and lived alone, died at her home on 15th November.

'She was a very private person, who never mixed business with pleasure,' Ms Taylor added, 'and she was a true gem. It's strange that she died on the 15th November. She always took that day off work as annual leave, and no-one ever knew why.'

When they finish reading the article, Sam and Maria sit very still for what seems like a long time. Eventually, Sam sighs loudly and clears his throat, while blinking back tears of sadness. He looks at Maria, her head bowed, tears rolling down her cheeks.

They are both so overcome with emotion, as they realise that Dr Nadia Selon has perhaps paid the ultimate emotional price for having had an illegitimate baby in 1960.

Acknowledgements

You must make a choice to take a chance, or your life will never change

Thanks for all those 'chance' conversations with so many people over the years while developing the idea of writing this book.

Christine and Indie Authors World, thank you for turning this dream into a reality. A chance opportunity led me to you, thereby enabling this story to come to life about the many forgotten women of the 1960s.

The choice was hard, but the risk prompted by my half-full glass approach to life made it possible. My passion, drive, and determination, and my love of life are endless. This book is something I would never in my wildest dreams have believed was possible

Last but not least, thank you to my family and friends – immediate and extended – for your love and support throughout my life.

Sometimes when life is at its hardest, that's when you grow the most. It's not what happened to Mafalda, it's what she did with what happened to her that mattered. I would say little Mafalda was a 'powerful battler', as her name depicts. Many children are born with the blueprint to survive. Little Mafalda was lucky enough to have Nadia, who gave her life and love even for a short period of time. Zoe was even luckier to have had such loving parents, who provided her with the opportunity and support to achieve her hopes and aspirations.

About The Author

Mairi Speirs is a lecturer in a further education college, she has always had a keen interest in how children, young people and families develop over time and the issues affecting them since gaining an SNNEB qualification in early education and childcare in the early 1980s.

This along with a keen interest in family structures formed the basis of this fictional short story along with a deep sadness for all women worldwide who had their babies forcibly taken from them.

She is married is a parent and a delighted gran of their growing family.

She also enjoys pursuing an interest in writing short stories during her holidays.

She is currently working on her 2nd short story the' Ebb and Flow of the Chromosome Trick' which also has a focus on children, young people and families and the topical issues affecting them.

Contact her at facebook.com/mairispeirsauthor